WALTZ WITH A STRANGER

Susan nearly collided with a tall gentleman in a black domino who had come up to where she was standing.

"I beg your pardon, ma'am. I trust I'm not intruding, but I hoped you might consent to dance this next set with me if you're not already engaged."

"Oh, yes, I should be very glad to dance with you," said Susan fervently.

As soon as Susan and the tall gentleman had taken their places on the floor, the fiddlers struck up a rollicking country dance. Susan and the tall gentleman led off, and for the first few minutes, neither of them spoke. When they had successfully gone down the line, however, and retired to a place lower on the floor, the tall gentleman cleared his throat and addressed Susan in an apologetic tone.

"Forgive me for being such a dull partner."

Susan gave him a deprecating smile. "I'm sorry that you were obliged to labor so hard on my account. It's infamous that you should have to wear yourself out rescuing me from my other partner. But I do appreciate your efforts on my behalf."

"It was nothing."

"Indeed, it was *not* nothing," said Susan warmly. "It was very generous of you to champion me as you did, and I assure you that I am extremely grateful for it. I only wish there was something I could do for you in return."

The tall gentleman looked down at Susan meditatively. "Do you?" he said. "That might be arranged, you know."

The way his eyes dwelt on Susan's lips told her exactly what kind of arrangement he had in mind. . . .

—from *Moonlight Masquerade* by Joy Reed

WATCH FOR THESE REGENCY ROMANCES

SPELLBOUND HEARTS

Jo Ann Ferguson
Karla Hocker
Joy Reed

Zebra Books
Kensington Publishing Corp.
http://www.zebrabooks.com

ZEBRA BOOKS are published by

Kensington Publishing Corp.
850 Third Avenue
New York, NY 10022

First Printing: October, 1997
10 9 8 7 6 5 4 3 2 1

Printed in the United States of America

CONTENTS

Spellbound

Jo Ann Ferguson

"I fear I don't know whom else I can turn to, Fayette."

Fayette Wychwood smiled. Her bosom-bow Venetia Tanner had exquisite skin, glorious black hair, and a gift for exaggerating every small disappointment into a disaster. "Venetia, you have so many friends."

"But none who can do what you can."

"What I can?" she repeated, sure she had misunderstood.

Venetia Tanner's tear-filled eyes widened as she whispered, "I know who you are and what you can do."

"You are making no sense."

"Aha!"

"Aha?"

"You are lying!" Venetia's laugh was weak but triumphant, as tears fell along her full cheeks. "You always blush as red as a rose when you are not being an honest trout. If you were dark-haired like me, instead of being as blond as honey, you would be able to conceal it." She laughed again. "But you cannot! And you are lying now."

Fayette clasped her hands in her lap. "I am a square person. You should not make such accusations."

"Unless they are true." She leaned forward on the settee in the middle of the simple parlor. "And 'tis true. You are blushing, so you know I am making perfect sense."

"You are prattling like a gabble-grinder. What sense is there in that?"

Venetia put her hands over Fayette's. All happiness left her voice as she moaned, "Don't hoax me now, I beg you. I need help desperately, Fayette, and you are the only one who can help me. I have met a man I cannot put from my mind."

"That is grand, but I do not understand what that has to do with me."

"It has much to do with you when I am uncertain if he returns my heartfelt affection." Her fingers tightened on Fayette's. "That is why I need your help. I want him to fall eternally in love with me. We met during the Little Season. I wish you had been there."

"But what does that have to do with me? I have never even been to Town."

"You should come for the Season."

"My family has never found a welcome among the Polite World."

Instead of commiserating with her as Fayette had expected, Venetia smiled and dashed the tears from her eyes. "Exactly!"

"Exactly?"

"That's exactly why I know you're the only one to help me. The *ton* has always been leery of your family and what you can do."

"What we can do?" she asked cautiously. She did not like the course of this conversation.

"I want you to put a spell on this gentleman to make him fall in love with me."

Fayette drew back from her friend. What had she said to betray herself? Mayhap it was nothing more than the stories bandied about whenever a firstborn Wychwood daughter left her childhood behind. No, she could not let herself become lost in wistful thinking, because Venetia would not have risked their friendship on something as unsubstantial as chit-chat.

"What you are asking . . ." she began.

"Is perfectly possible for you. I know." Venetia lowered her voice to a conspiratorial murmur as she wiped yet another tear from her eye. "I saw what you did in the garden last week."

"What I did?"

"I saw you with a piece of rock in your hand and how you held it up to the sky. I could not hear what you said, but I watched how the clouds billowed up and it began to rain." She asked in a whisper, "What was it?"

"Simply a rock," she hedged.

"What sort of rock?"

"A piece of lava. Captain Morrison brought it back to my great-aunt after one of his voyages to the South Pacific."

Venetia waved that fact aside. "Wherever you got it, it was magical! And if you can do something like that, you must have an incantation to make a man fall in love with me."

Fayette sank back against her chair. How many times had Mama warned her not to play with the spells Auntie Delphina Wychwood had taught her in the still hours before dawn?

"That was different," she whispered. If Auntie Delphina overheard this conversation, there would be the devil to pay and no pitch hot.

"Magic is magic." Venetia's lower lip trembled. "And if you do not help me, I swear I shall pine away and die of a broken heart."

"Do not be absurd."

"My sister died of a broken heart. My cousin died of a broken heart. Why not me?"

Fayette hesitated. It was true that everyone in the shire said the Tanner women had turned love into folderols and had withered away when their hearts found no home in the breasts of the men they adored. Everyone, that is, save Auntie Delphina, who had warned them that their deaths had less to do with broken hearts and more to do with the belladonna they used to paint their faces and the laudanum they had swallowed to ease their vapors.

If Venetia turned to the weak-hearted ways of her family . . . Fayette sighed. The spell to make a man fall in love with a woman who loved him was such a simple one. What could it hurt? Auntie Delphina had told her it worked only if two hearts were inclined toward love already.

"You must tell no one I am doing this for you," she said, glancing at the door. "I do not want the world and its brother coming to my doorstep and asking me to bring lonely hearts together."

"Then you can do it? You can truly do it?"

"I believe I can. All you need to do is retrieve some fresh soil from where this gentleman has stepped."

"Me?" Venetia shook her head, dashing tears from her eyes. "I cannot do such a thing."

"But—"

"Fayette, you must do it. You are the one who has the gift of magic. And if he were to see me . . . Alack! How would I explain myself?"

"But if this is a London gentleman, you cannot expect me to go there and gather the soil."

"He lives near here." Venetia glanced away, dabbing her eyes with her handkerchief.

Fayette hesitated, then, as her friend began to weep again, she sighed. "All right. I will get the soil. When I give it to you, you must plant it along with a flower in a pot you can keep close to you during the day and especially during the night. Talk to the plant and offer it warmth as you would your gentleman. Soon he will present himself and his heart."

Venetia grasped her hands and squeezed them as tears flowed down her cheeks again. "Oh, my dear

Fayette, I believe you can make this happen. If you do, I shall be the most grateful, happy woman this world has ever seen."

She ignored her friend's exaggeration, too accustomed, after their years of friendship, to her embellishment of every feeling. "Who is your gentleman?"

"Jeremiah St. James."

"St. James?" she gulped, fighting the urge to look out the cottage's window toward the huge manor house crouched on the hill above this small house where she lived with her widowed mother and her maiden greataunt. Although, or mayhap because, their lands were joined at a simple stone wall, the St. James family had long been the nemesis of her family. Her earliest memories included warnings to stay far from the estate and its denizens.

"Yes," Venetia replied, clearly choosing to ignore Fayette's shock. "Isn't it amazing? I grew up less than a league from his home, but we never met until this past Little Season. Jeremiah St. James was the smartest man in town, and I cannot forget him."

"So you said before," Fayette said, glad her voice remained even. *But I want nothing to do with anyone named St. James.* "Venetia, on second thought, I cannot help you."

"Fayette, you promised!"

Sighing again, she wondered why she had let her friend corner her once more. By the elevens, she knew Venetia well enough. She should have suspected something was amiss when Venetia had been reticent about her gentleman's name.

"So I did," she murmured. Still not looking out the window at the forbidding house, she added, "Tell me what Jeremiah St. James looks like."

The request was a mistake, Fayette knew, when Venetia began to list off each of her beloved's attributes. No man could possibly be more handsome, more generous, more intelligent, more . . . Fayette stopped listening to what a paragon he was. Otherwise, she was not sure she could resist the tempting thought of adding another small incantation to the spell so the inimitable Mr. St. James would sneeze for an hour. No, she could not do that, because she must think only generous thoughts while working this charm for Venetia. Otherwise, she risked having harmful thoughts bounced back on her.

When Venetia left, bubbling over with all the plans she must make before the banns were read, Fayette went up the stairs to her bedchamber. The spell was simple, but preparations needed to be made. First, she had to get a handful of dirt bearing Mr. St. James's boot print.

She paused at the top of the stairs and stared out the window at the massive house that seemed as ancient as the rocks it had been built upon. Devil a bit! Had she been born beneath a midsummer moon to agree to help Venetia? She would have to climb over the stone wall and cross the fields where she had been warned never to walk. She was a widgeon to start upon this totty-headed scheme. Too soft a heart and too soft a head would be Auntie Delphina's opinion, but Fayette never had been able to remain unmoved by a friend's tears.

Soft footsteps crossed the hall behind her, and she turned to see Mrs. Jennings. The stocky housekeeper wore a scowl in place of her customary smile. Wagging a gnarled finger, she reached in front of Fayette and drew the curtains closed.

"Miss Fayette, I hope I heard wrong."

Fayette tried to ignore the claws suddenly scratching at her stomach. When Mrs. Jennings owned to eavesdropping, it was only because the housekeeper was too distressed by what she had overheard to remain silent.

"Did I hear you speak to Miss Tanner about performing a love spell for her?" Mrs. Jennings continued. "You know better than to promise such things."

"Venetia needed some hope."

Mrs. Jennings shook her head. "But you told your mother that you would never attempt such a thing."

Turning away, Fayette avoided catching her guilty reflection in the glass by her bedchamber door. Yes, she had promised Mama to forget all that she had learned, the legacy of her father's family from the moment time began. *But why do we share this knowledge with each other and deny it to those who need us?*

As if she had spoken aloud, Mrs. Jennings continued, "You know what trouble your great-great-great grandmother found herself in when she was jobbernowl enough to reveal what she could do."

"That was ages ago."

"Not so long ago," the gray-haired woman said coldly as she followed Fayette into the simple bedchamber.

"Times change."

"True, but people do not. Those that are afraid will try to destroy those that dare."

Fayette sat on the chaise longue at the foot of the unadorned bed. Although she was spare in height, her head brushed the sloping ceiling. She looked up at Mrs. Jennings, who stood in the middle of the room with her arms folded severely across her full shelf of chest.

"But I promised Venetia," Fayette argued. "Surely, just this once, with this one modest spell, there should be no problem."

Mrs. Jennings's frown did not ease. "I pray you are right."

Fayette wished she could be anywhere but here. Here on the grounds of Saint's Rest, the home of the St. James family. As she had clambered over the stone wall in a manner better befitting a child than a young woman, her silly fear that wickedness would sweep out and obliterate her grew even stronger. A Wychwood woman never, never, never stepped foot on St. James's property.

Yet here she was. She did not want to own, not even to herself, that a hint of impish curiosity had as much as friendship to do with her promise to help Venetia.

What was it about this estate that Auntie Delphina refused to speak of? Auntie Delphina had no trouble sharing all the tittle-tattle from the village down by the stream. She loved to whisper the gossip she had heard at the market day near the crossroads. After every fair and festival in the shire, Auntie Delphina came home with the latest *on dits*.

But she never spoke of why Fayette should stay far from this estate. Surely Old Scratch himself could not have taken up an earthly residence here on this hill that was drenched in sunlight and the last of the season's wildflowers. Horrible things might have happened in the past, but that was when ignorance ruled, not like now in the second decade of the nineteenth century.

Fayette hurried through the open meadow. No one halted her as she left the leas behind and entered the carefully cultivated gardens. She found a hummock beneath a tree whose leaves were a brilliant gold. Sitting with a small, wooden cup on her knees, she prepared to wait.

A horse riding neck-or-nothing up the long alley edged with ancient trees caught her attention. She sat straighter when she noted that the man atop the steed had ebony hair. Could this be the dashing swain who had stolen Venetia's heart?

Squinting into the sunshine, she realized the rider was on his way to the stables between her and the house which was half hidden by a small copse. Perfect! She stood and hurried up the hill toward the low buildings that had been constructed of the same gray stone as the house. Being careful that no one saw her, she edged closer to the stable.

Hearty voices greeted the rider as she pressed against the stable wall that stank with the decaying greenery that had already given up its life at the end of summer. She frowned as a rough stone caught on her gown. Bending to free the snag, she peeked around the corner to see the rider dismount onto the cobbles in front of the stable.

This had to be Mr. St. James, for he fit the description Venetia had given her as surely as Fayette's favorite slippers fit her toes. It was a shame he was the younger brother, for he had a lordly mien. His black hair glistened like water in the bottom of a well on the night of a full moon. The high collar he wore beneath his riding coat could not hide the firm line of his jaw. When she noted the grace, yet strength in each motion, she understood why Venetia pined for this man. He was, without question, the most handsome man Fayette had ever seen, and he possessed an aura of power that warned others to approach only at their own risk.

As she must.

Taking a deep breath to gird herself, she waited for the stableboy to lead the chestnut horse into the stable. She inched past the stable door. Looking around the far corner, she sighed. The cobbles continued toward the house. An excellent idea to keep the mud of the yard outside, but it ill-served her purpose of gathering up some earth that held the print of his boots. If he walked directly to the house, she might have to return home without the soil she needed.

The lilt of a whistle teased her ears, and she smiled as she recognized the song. Auntie Delphina had taught her the same cheerful tune years ago. That someone of the St. James family knew it as well eased the fear that had haunted her since she had agreed to cross the stone wall onto these lands. No monsters lived here, only a family that had preyed on hers in ignorance in the past.

She wanted to shout with joy when Mr. St. James turned from the walkway leading to the copse and into another grove of trees that separated the stables from a rose garden. Finally! Now, she could begin her work before someone noticed her. She had had such good fortune so far. As Auntie Delphina would say, fortune smiled most readily on those trying to help others.

Her high-lows sank into the damp grass as she tried not to step on any of the recently fallen leaves. The crunch might alert Mr. St. James to the fact he was being pursued. She had not expected such a perfect mantle of greenery decorated with the golds and scarlets of autumn beneath the trees in this small copse. The lush blanket urged her to forget what she had come here to do as she reclined back in it and listened to the song-birds above in the brightly colored leaves. So often Auntie Delphina had said that one should heed the sounds around one and savor the blessings that came from the earth each day.

She heard Mr. St. James shout a greeting to someone she could not see. She paid neither the words nor the response any mind as she stared down at the damp earth in front of her. It had been overturned not long ago, mayhap for planting more of the flowers edging the trees or mayhap by an animal rooting in the ground. The reason mattered far less than the fact that in front of her was the perfect imprint of Mr. St. James's riding boot.

She bent to scoop the dirt into her cup. Closing her eyes, she whispered the words that would set the incantation in place, "Let this be the beginning of a love that—"

"Who are you, and what are you doing?"

At the male voice, Fayette froze, save for her eyes which slowly rose along the unsullied boots and the dark breeches to the scarlet riding coat and past the uncompromising chin to the most startling blue eyes she had ever seen. She suspected they sparked like the heart of a flame when they were bright with merriment, but no sign of mirth lessened their intensity as he stared down at her.

Thinking as quickly as she could when that cobalt gaze held her, she said, "Sir, I am sorry to have intruded, but I found myself drawn to admire these beautiful flowers. I have not seen their like before." As heat rose up her cheeks, she prayed her bonnet would hide the damning flush that betrayed every goose's gazette she spoke.

"Drawn from the road which is a good quarter mile away?" His voice was a sublime tenor that suited the jolly song he had been whistling, but no levity filled it now.

"No."

"Mayhap from the house? Are you a guest within whom I have failed to be informed about?"

"No." She wished lying was not so impossible for her, because now certainly would be the time for an out-and-outer or two. If her cheeks became as crimson as the leaves, he would surely guess she was being false.

He flung out a hand. "Do you wish me to believe you have just appeared here as if by magic?"

"Of course not." She laughed, then wished she had not, when the sound was strained like the dirt sifting through her fingers.

Holding out his hand in a command, he was silent. She considered ignoring it, but that was impossible when his long fingers were only inches from her nose. Dismay ached within her as she realized she must devise some excuse for being here. Some excuse that was the truth, yet not the truth. Nothing she said or did must link her to Venetia Tanner. A single wrong word now could ruin any hopes her friend had of winning this man's heart, although why sweet Venetia, who would not say boo to a goose, was so utterly taken with this man, who was as forbidding as his ancestral home, might be the greatest mystery of all.

Fayette imprisoned her sigh behind her tightly clamped lips as she placed the wooden cup on his hand. He glanced from it to her, puzzlement stealing the hard edge from his face. For a moment, as he looked as confused as a young lad, she could understand why Venetia had lost her heart to him.

But only for a moment, because his voice remained arrogant. "You are a most peculiar thief, miss, for I cannot recall anyone ever sneaking into Saint's Rest to steal dirt. Or mayhap you are digging here in search of some treasure long forgotten by my family?"

"It is not easy to explain."

"I am certain it is not." He offered his other hand. "However, I am equally certain that I would find this conversation easier if you were not kneeling in the dirt like a beggar. I would accuse you of being one, but I suspect anyone in such need would come to the kitchen door as lief lurking in the gardens collecting dirt."

She put her fingers on his hand to let him assist her to her feet. She rued the motion as soon as his flesh surrounded hers. Even as her skin tingled with some unknown sensation, something flickered through his eyes. Slowly he brought her up, drawing her a half step closer.

His gaze swept over her from the top of her bonnet that sat on her blond hair to the tip of her boots peeking out from beneath the lace edging her light blue gown. When his mouth quirked, she clenched her fists at her side. She knew her clothes were not *à la modality* as

Venetia's were, but he need not laugh at her country-put ways.

"Who are you?" he asked as his stare returned to meet hers. "I have not seen you here before."

"I haven't been here before."

"You are visiting from London?"

"No, I live here in the shire." She took a step back to put more space between them. "I simply have not been at Saint's Rest before."

"I suppose you have had no reason to call when no one has been in residence but the servants who have kept the house and grounds from ruin." He smiled as he grasped her hand once more. Lifting it, he did not press it to his lips as he said, "I trust that will change now that I have returned to oversee the legacy my father left in the hands of my brother and me." He turned her hand over. "Although I must own, I find it much more pleasurable to have you in my hands just now."

Fayette had no idea how to answer, as his thumb stroked her palm. If she were to own the truth, she wished only to snatch the cup containing the earth from him and to flee, never to come back. The caress of his rough skin against her fingers, his warm smile, his enigmatic eyes . . . They all sent a peculiar excitement racing through her which both unsettled her and made her want to sing that joyous song he had been whistling.

"As we have not met previously, allow me to introduce myself." He bowed over her hand again. "Cassidy St. James, miss."

"*Cassidy* St. James? I thought you were . . ." She was making a bumble-bath of the whole of this.

He chuckled. "Don't fret. 'Tis a common mistake Jeremiah and I have learned to endure since his birth only minutes after mine."

"You are twins?"

"I thought I just said that."

Fayette wanted to groan. She should have remembered that the old lord had been blessed with twin boys, although no one mentioned this family within her home. The celebration of that event had been so grand that it was spoken of even after her own birth five years later. That the brothers had been away at school and then in town up until now was no excuse for her ignorance. Why hadn't Venetia warned her that both brothers had come down from London?

"And who, I ask for what must be, at the very least, the third time, are you?" he went on when she remained silent.

"Fayette Wychwood, my lord." She pointed through the trees toward her house that was nearly lost beyond the rolling hills. "I live along the road in that direction."

His eyes widened. "Wychwood?" A grin added a macabre light to his face, for the amusement did not reach his eyes. "I should have guessed."

"Guessed what?"

"Now you cannot expect me to believe you haven't heard the tales whispered throughout the village about your family and the strange antics you embark upon."

"Of course I have heard the tales of my family as well as the tales of yours." She rushed to add when his brows dipped in a scowl, "But I give no credence to poker-talk. I am surprised you do, my lord."

"I seldom heed it." He held up the cup. "But don't you consider it more than a bit odd that you are collecting dirt in a wooden chalice?"

"No."

"No? Do you know that is a most unsatisfactory answer when I am waiting for an explanation of your most outlandish behavior?"

Again she found herself at a loss. What could she say that was the truth, so she did not blush, yet would not tip him off to Venetia's plans for his brother?

Inspiration came as she glanced once more at the roof of the cottage where she lived with Mama and Auntie Delphina. "I don't know about how you shall deem my answer, my lord, but I do know that, in 1555, Enid Wychwood was found guilty of being in league with the devil because she was able to cure a local farmer's sheep."

"What has that to do with this?"

"Let me finish. The man who oversaw her hanging, and who wanted to dominate the wool industry in this shire, was named Lord St. James."

"1555? That would have been Andrew St. James, I suspect. He made a fortune in wool and obtained the queen's good graces on our family. I believe he was the first earl." He handed her back the cup. "Your point, however, is well, albeit belatedly, taken. Things may not be always as they seem. Gathering a bit of earth is not necessarily a prelude to some enchantment."

"True." *Although this time, it is.* Holding the cup to her chest, she said, "I bid you good day, my lord."

"Good day to you, Miss Wychwood." She was not sure if she heard amusement or a threat in his voice as he added, "I trust I shall see you soon."

"Oh, dear. Oh, dear. Oh, dear."

"Will you please say something else?" Fayette had rushed to Venetia's house in the village after her encounter with Lord St. James. She had hoped coming to call on Venetia would offer some insight into this jumble. Instead, her friend could do nothing, save wringing her hands and worrying the lace on the front of her morning dress that was the same pale green as the sitting room walls.

This elegant country home was as different from Fayette's simple cottage as Saint's Rest. Velvet-footed servants did not loiter by the doors to listen, so they might chide Venetia later. The pieces of furniture had been chosen to complement the room and each other.

"Oh, my," moaned Venetia. "Oh, my. Oh—"

"No, no, no!" Fayette cried. "That was not what I meant. Why did you say nothing to me about Cassidy St. James?"

With a shiver, Venetia whispered, "I had prayed he would remain far, far from here until I could win Jeremiah's heart. He is the devil himself."

"Which one? Lord St. James or Mr. St. James?"

"Fayette!" Outrage snapped in her eyes. "You should not speak of my dear Jeremiah that way, even in jest."

"It was no jest." Rising, she went to the window overlooking the garden which was withering in the October chill. "After encountering Lord St. James, I am right to be curious about his brother."

"They are nothing alike."

Fayette turned and arched a brow. "Then you, Venetia, misled me with your description of your beloved."

Coming to her feet, Venetia drew another lacy handkerchief from her bodice. Two others lay, sodden and forgotten, on the settee. She dabbed her eyes before whispering, "You are right. They are alike in appearance, but in nothing else. Where Jeremiah is warm and kind, his brother is cold and callous."

"Cold?" She resisted the urge to laugh. Although his manner had been imperious, Lord St. James had not been cold. The fire in his eyes could sear the strongest soul, and his smile easily enticed one to listen to the words he twisted with such ease.

"Fayette, forgive me. I had not guessed you would be forced to confront him. I am only grateful you escaped unscathed."

"He was not ill-mannered to me."

"Truly?"

"Not overly ill-mannered."

Venetia sobbed again into her handkerchief.

"Do not weep," Fayette murmured, even though she knew, from past experience, how futile such words were. "I am fine."

"But . . ." She picked up the cup of earth and tilted it to let the soil dribble out into a planter by the settee. "All is lost."

"Mayhap not."

"Mayhap not?" Venetia's eyes brightened.

Fayette spoke her prayers backward under her breath. Had she been on the wrong side of the hedge when brains were passed out? She should let this end here.

"Mayhap not?" Venetia prompted impatiently.

"Give me a day or two to ponder what we might do."

"Then I shall win the heart of my darling Jeremiah." Her smile became predatory. "Whether Lord St. James wishes it or not."

"The earl does not want his brother courting you?" That was a shock, because Venetia was a diamond of birth.

"No, but we shall defeat him, shan't we, Fayette?"

Again she had the opportunity to get herself out of this shocking mull. She could not. Not when she had the chance to tweak the St. James family's collective nose. It would be small retribution for the past, but it might be all she could get.

"Yes," she said with a smile, "we shall defeat him."

Fayette was late for supper, which obtained her a scowl from Mrs. Jennings and a reprimand from Mama. Auntie Delphina, who was sitting in her customary place at the head of the table in the cramped dining room, simply motioned for Fayette to take her seat.

Glad no one had asked her why she was delayed, because she did not want to own she had been reading the ancient books that Auntie Delphina kept in the tiny room at the back of the attic, Fayette hurried to her chair. She smiled at Mama who sat across the mahogany table.

Mama still possessed the beauty that had won Papa's heart from the moment he saw her walking along a Cambridge street. He had courted her, winning her affection and the affection of her family, including her father who once had lectured at the university. Her hair was now more silver than gold, but her eyes were a warm blue.

"I understand you gave our neighbors a look-in today, Fayette," Auntie Delphina said as she passed the soup tureen to Mama. She glanced at Mrs. Jennings who stood in the corner, and Fayette knew exactly where her father's aunt had heard about her trip across the stone wall.

"The Aylesworths?" Mama asked, ladling out the vegetable soup. "How is dear Mrs. Aylesworth?"

"I am sure she is doing better now that the baby is weaned." Fayette waited for Mama to pass the tureen. Her hours in the fresh, crisp autumn air had honed her appetite.

Auntie Delphina arched a single, snowy brow. " 'Twas my understanding you did not call on the Aylesworths, Fayette, but our other neighbors."

The spoon clattered against the tureen as Mama's face became as pale as Auntie Delphina's hair. "You cannot be intimating that Fayette went *there.*"

"I was not intimating. I was stating the truth." She leaned her elbow on the table and pierced Fayette with a glower. "Isn't it the truth that you went across the stone wall onto Saint's Rest lands this afternoon?"

"Oh, dear God in heaven," whispered Mama.

Fayette had learned long ago it was useless to lather

Auntie Delphina with balms. Mama might believe her, but Auntie Delphina saw things no one else could discern. Even if Fayette did not blush, Auntie Delphina would know she was lying.

"Yes," she answered as she tried to spoon soup into her bowl without her trembling fingers spilling any, "I went for a walk through the St. James's fields. The trees were so beautiful in their autumn colors."

"But they are beautiful here. Why did you have to go *there*?" Mama moaned, her blue eyes dim with despair. Stretching across the table, she seized Fayette's hand. "Think what might have happened if someone from that family were at home."

"I shudder to think." Now that, Fayette knew was the truth.

Mama closed her eyes and moaned again. "I should never have let Edward make me promise to come to this horrible place after his death."

"You had nowhere else to go," Aunt Delphina said in her no-nonsense voice. "A young widow with a small pension and a baby is welcome on few doorsteps."

"But now . . ." Mama's voice strengthened as she gripped Fayette's hand more tightly. "My dear, dear child, you must never wander onto the St. James's estate again. It is too dangerous for you."

Auntie Delphina picked up a piece of bread and offered the plate to Mama. "For once, we are in complete agreement."

"Have you seen something?" The awe in Mama's voice was tinged with envy that she could never perceive what often seemed so clear to both her husband's aunt and her daughter. "Do tell us, for Fayette must be warned before she does something out of hand."

Reaching, Auntie Delphina took Fayette's hand and turned it palm up. "The answer is here as it has been in the hands of every firstborn daughter who bears the

Wychwood name. To enter that estate has been, generation after generation, the greatest hazard a firstborn
Wychwood daughter can take upon herself."

"What sort of danger?" Mama gasped before Fayette
could.

Auntie Delphina ran her nail along Fayette's palm,
then released her hand. Fayette stared into it, wondering what Auntie Delphina had seen that she could not,
for this skill of reading the future within the lines im-
printed in a person's hand was one she did not possess.

"Beware, Fayette," Auntie Delphina murmured. "You
have gone there once and have found your way home,
but you may not be granted such fortune again."

"What do you mean?" she asked.

"If you go there again, your life as you have lived it
here will be over. You will put every part of you in peril
from which you might never escape."

"Oh, dear God in heaven!" Mama swayed and
swooned against the back of her chair.

Fayette leaped to her feet, running to cradle Mama
before she could slip to the floor. "Mrs. Jennings! *Sal
volatile!*"

"Yes, miss!" For once, the housekeeper did not give
her any back-talk.

"Mama?" She glanced over her shoulder to where
Auntie Delphina was dipping her spoon into her soup.
"How can you be so calm?"

"She is coming about."

Fayette looked down, knowing her great-aunt was always right in situations like this. Mama's eyelashes flut-
tered against her porcelain cheeks, and she moaned
softly.

"Mrs. Jennings!" Fayette called. "Bring a damp cloth
to put on Mama's forehead."

"Straightaway, Miss Fayette."

Mama grasped Fayette's hand again and whispered, "My dear, dear child, promise me."

"Anything, Mama."

Auntie Delphina muttered, "Be careful what you offer, Fayette."

Mama either did not or chose not to hear her late husband's aunt. Still gripping Fayette's hand, she said in the same fragile voice, "Promise me that you will avoid Lord St. James."

"Why not ask her to bring you the moon and the stars?" grumbled the old woman who was eating her soup with gusto. "With the lad just across the field, do you think he will ignore a lovely lass like her?"

Fayette knew Mama had heard that, because her lips grew rigid as she demanded, "Delphina, how can you be just sitting there and eating at a time like this?"

"It *is* supper time."

"But our dear Fayette may be in mortal danger."

Aunt Delphina gave Fayette a steady look up and down. "I suspect it is not mortal danger she needs fear. From what I have heard, the St. James lads have cut quite a swath through the Polite World, leaving a trail of broken hearts after them."

"I had not heard that," Fayette said as she stepped back to allow Mrs. Jennings to hand the damp cloth to Mama.

"You should listen," Auntie Delphina chided, "more closely to the *on dits* in the village. Some prattle is actually true."

She went back around the table to her chair. So easily she could imagine Lord St. James winning a woman's heart, for he had a rakish way about him. Yet, he possessed a gallantry that was at odds with a man who would prevail upon a woman's heart and then toss it aside to shatter in grief. He had contested her in a battle of words, but had accepted defeat gracefully and with a sense of humor that she found utterly captivating.

Mama moaned again. "This is your fault, Delphina. If you had not taught her all that sorcery—"

Putting down her spoon, Delphina grew serious. "It is because I feared this very situation might come about that I have taught Fayette to protect herself from the wickedness that stalks this shire. I have taught her all I know."

"And that is what worries me," Mama murmured.

"So what will we do now?" Venetia retied the ribbons on her stylish bonnet and folded her arms on the gate in front of the Wychwood house.

Fayette opened the gate and her parasol at the same time. A walk along the lane today in this glorious sunshine should be the perfect antidote to her dismals. "I cannot go back there."

"You must!"

"Auntie Delphina said—"

Venetia leaned forward, anticipation heightening her voice. "What did that old witch say?"

"Venetia!"

Her friend had the decency to wear a rare flush. "Forgive me, Fayette. I know you have a great affection for your great-aunt, but I am so disappointed. I must convince Jeremiah St. James to fall in love with me."

"Then you shall have to use your own charms. Mine will not work now."

"But—"

Hoofbeats came at a perilous pace along the road that contorted up the hill from the village. Venetia screamed in horror as a pair of horses bore down on them. Fayette snatched Venetia's arm and pulled her back through the gate.

Two horses stopped in a cloud of dust that made Fayette sneeze once, twice, three times. Was this her punishment for daring to imagine putting such a curse on Mr. St. James? She was just being silly. She was sneezing because two riders, who must have been born at Hogs Norton, did not have the decency to ride at a prudent pace along the lane.

Irritation whetted her voice. "Are you all about in the head to ride like that? What if a child had been in your path?"

"I daresay we would have skirted it."

At the voice, which had echoed in her head since her visit to Saint's Rest, Fayette blinked away the dust in her eyes to discover Lord St. James dismounting from the back of the chestnut she had seen him riding before.

"We meet again, Miss Wychwood," he continued, "although one might not recognize you without that winsome dab of dirt shadowing your cheek."

She put her hand to her face, then pulled her fingers hastily away when he grinned. Her retort went unspoken when she realized, for the first time, his smile was mirrored in his eyes, dazzling and beguiling.

"And this," he said, motioning to the other man, "is my brother Jeremiah, who has urged me to stop by during our ride and atone for quizzing you when I encountered you at Saint's Rest."

"Quizzing you so unmercifully," his brother replied as he swung down from his gray dappled horse. Facing them, he smiled. "Allow me to present myself properly. Jeremiah St. James, Miss Wychwood."

Fayette heard Venetia's soft intake of breath as she stared at the brothers standing side by side. Both possessed those startling, blue eyes and the aquiline nose that gave them the same devilish good looks. Yet, only on first glance were they identical, for Jeremiah was taller by a finger's breadth. Where Lord St. James's broad shoulders narrowed along his torso to his muscular legs, his brother was a square block of flesh.

And, in other ways, they were different. Ways that could not be sensed with the eyes, but with the sense Auntie Delphina had helped her discover. Gentle, warm light encircled Jeremiah while his brother was draped in shades of gold and blue. Fayette could not pull her gaze from that glow, which should be a warning to put an end to this conversation with all due haste. Such a glow warned of a man of rare intelligence and strength, a man who saw few shades of gray and might be as unwilling to accept the unfamiliar as his ancestors had been.

"It is a pleasure, Mr. St. James," she managed to say when she realized the silence would be broken only with her reply. "You know my friend Venetia Tanner, if I am not mistaken."

"You are not. My dear Miss Tanner, I am so delighted to see you again." Mr. St. James's eyes warmed as he turned to take Venetia's hand. He bent to bring it to his lips.

Why, Fayette wondered, had Venetia come to her weeping and pleading for her assistance when it was obvious Mr. St. James returned her tender feelings?

That answer came like a thunderbolt out of a clear sky when Lord St. James stepped forward and said, "It is, indeed, an unexpected pleasure to see you again here in daisyville, Miss Tanner. Jeremiah, you should not have kept the fact that Miss Tanner's family has a residence nearby to Saint's Rest a secret from me."

His brother became as still as a statue, before releasing Venetia's hand as if it had been doused with something distasteful. Mr. St. James backed away, almost tripping over his own feet in his haste.

"Excuse me," he mumbled. "Thirsty. Getting a drink."

Fayette watched in amazement while he lurched to the well by the side of the cottage and drew up a bucket. Next to her, Venetia gulped a sob as she gazed after him. Turning, Fayette saw the earl's uneasy expression which was focused on his brother as well. She wanted to demand that just one of the trio explain what was amiss.

She hoped it was not what her eyes were showing her. If Mr. St. James were so easily governed by his brother, there must be a reason. Did Mr. St. James fear his brother? She looked back at Lord St. James. His taut face warned he was struggling to restrain his reaction, but restrain what? His temper? His dismay? His jealousy?

At that thought, something pricked her so sharply over her heart that she looked down to see if a pin had escaped her hair to jab her. She put her fingers on her bodice and forced a slow breath. Now was, unquestionably, not the time to act skimble-skamble. She should not care a brass button if Venetia Tanner had caught Lord St. James's eye.

Fayette said into the silence, "You may make your amends now, my lord, if you wish."

"Or how I wish?"

"I don't understand."

He smiled as he plucked one of the late chrysanthemums from the flower bed beside the gate. Holding it out to her, he said, "I think you do. I think you understand many, many things you would as lief not own to."

"Your opinion, not mine."

"Not mine alone." Tossing the blossom to her, he chuckled when she caught it. "Instead of an apology, Miss Wychwood, I would like to strike a bargain with you."

"What sort of bargain?"

"You are always suspicious of my motives when I have given you no cause to be." He stepped toward her. When she did not back away, astonishment stole the amusement from his face. His voice became somber. "I am not the one raised in a family whose members have been accused throughout time for doing the devil's work."

"I thought you did not heed rumors."

"It would be easier to pay them no mind if you were not so devilishly pretty, Miss Wychwood."

Fire scored her cheeks, and she knew she was blushing. How dare he try to enchant her when she guessed he did not mean a single word of his compliments! And in front of his brother and Venetia, too!

"I shall not bargain with you, my lord."

"Why not?"

"Because in the fifteenth century—"

He grimaced. "Another history lesson? I cannot believe you are going to tell me another story from our families' merged past."

"Why not?"

"Last time you regaled me with an impromptu lecture, you knew the exact date."

She frowned at his sarcasm. "To own the truth, I do this time as well. It was a January Saturday in 1421 when Eveline Wychwood was banished from the village and left to die on the leas. No one would risk giving her shelter or food, so she froze to death."

"And upon whom should we place culpability for such a thoughtless, evil act?" He rested his arm on the saddle. "Dare I assume the blackguard had the name of St. James?"

"James St. James, who accused her of putting a spell on his family at the birth of his fifth daughter. Before her birth, he had bragged throughout England that the babe would finally be the male heir he craved. He accused Eveline after he had offered her a reward for bringing his son safely into the world." Tilting her parasol so she could return his superior smile, she said, "I trust you will see the lesson to be learned in that as well, my lord."

"You don't trust me."

"Not you personally. Everyone in your family."

He nodded coolly. "Then I would be wise to take my leave without further ado. Jeremiah?"

His brother stared at Fayette in awe as he went to his horse. Was it because of the whisper of witchcraft or because he had never seen anyone defy Lord St. James? She did not care. She just wanted them gone. If Venetia wished to entangle her life with these men, that was her choice, but Fayette wanted both of the St. James brothers to brush and lope with all speed.

Her eyes widened when Lord St. James swung into the saddle with more difficulty than she had expected. She was even more surprised when his brother asked, "Is that leg bothering you again, Cassidy?"

" 'Tis nothing," he returned so sharply the words sliced into her even though they were aimed at Mr. St. James. "You worry too much."

"I do." A hint of laughter echoed beneath his words. "I wish to keep you healthy."

"And alive."

"True, for then I would have the odious burden of being the earl."

Lord St. James clapped his brother on the shoulder and smiled broadly. When his glance caught Fayette's, that smile vanished as if it had never existed. A flush rose beneath his bronzed skin. Could he be embarrassed that she and Venetia had been witnesses to his affection for his brother?

His brother was not so circumspect. As he settled himself in the saddle, he said, "Cassidy hates being a hero."

"You were in the war, my lord?" Venetia asked, startling Fayette, because she had not heard her friend speak one word to the earl. Then she realized it was simply that Venetia would dare anything, even Lord St. James, to concoct a reason for Jeremiah to linger a moment longer.

"No."

Fayette put her arm around her friend's shoulders as Venetia recoiled. She had no chance to speak before Lord St. James called for his brother to follow and raced away along the road toward Saint's Rest.

"Pay him no mind," Mr. St. James said. "He is too modest." He sighed. "But it is not my place to explain." He tipped his hat to them. "I bid you good day, ladies."

As soon as Mr. St. James was riding away, Venetia ran to the well. She bent and scooped up a handful of dirt.

"Quick, Fayette. Bring me one of those flowerpots over by the gate."

"This may not be a good idea under the circumstances."

Venetia scowled and strode to get one of the pots. Carefully she put the small clump of earth into the clay pot. Smiling, she held it out to Fayette. "Opportunity often comes when and where we least expect it. Do what you must."

Fayette shook her head and handed it back. "If you insist on continuing with this, do as I told you. Plant a flower within it and tend it well as you think with affection of Mr. St. James."

"That will be easy." Her smile vanished. "But what if this soil was from beneath *his* boots?"

"His?"

"Lord St. James. With both of them here . . ." Venetia shuddered as she glanced toward the gate as if expecting something evil to come flying through it.

"Only Mr. St. James went to the well."

"So there is no chance I might use the earth for a plant and find that *he* comes calling?"

She put her hand on her friend's quivering arm.

"Venetia, you must rid yourself of this fear of Lord St. James."

"I am not the only one to be frightened of him."

"Who else is in such awe of him?" *In addition to me,* she added silently.

"You saw how Jeremiah reacted when his brother spoke to me."

"And I saw how he reacted when his brother spoke to him. Mr. St. James is not afraid of the earl. They respect each other."

"Respect may not be the exact word I would have chosen."

Exasperation gnawed at her. "Venetia, how can you expect to marry the younger brother and live with him as man and wife if you cannot bear to be beneath his older brother's roof?"

Venetia shook off Fayette's hand as they entered the cottage's small kitchen. "I have considered that question deeply for the past two days. The answer is quite simple. When the earl is in town, we will pay a visit here to grassville. If the earl wishes to ride to the hounds or have a country house gathering at Saint's Rest, we shall be busy in London. See how simple it is?"

"And has Jeremiah agreed to this?" She drew off her soiled gloves and put them beside the ones Auntie Delphina must have been using, for a second pair of gloves were ingrained with dirt.

"He will."

"I am not as certain as you are. He seems very fond of his brother."

Venetia patted the flowerpot. "But he shall be much fonder of me as soon as your magic touches his heart."

"Shh!" She rushed to the kitchen door and threw it open. If anyone beyond the household were to be listening at the door, tales of witchcraft would soon again be in the air. With Lord St. James at home, she must do nothing more to bring the ancient curse down upon her.

Or had she done too much already?

Cassidy watched in appreciative silence. In the years he had been away from Saint's Rest he had forgotten the stories that once he and Jeremiah had whispered beneath the covers when their governess thought they were long asleep. Tales of things that could not be explained away at the time, but things that had happened, witnessed by the most sober resident of the shire. Tales that always included the name Wychwood. Mistress Dyna Wychwood, who had been hunted through the greenwoods by a mob of angry villagers more than two hundred years before and accused of putting a curse upon the church so the roof collapsed. Beatrice Wychwood, a century before that, who was burned in retaliation for all who died after drinking from the village well near her door. Cybele Wychwood's story was even older than that, for she been labelled the devil's consort after she survived a fire, unhurt, that left half the village dead.

He grinned wryly as he recalled how he and Jeremiah had trembled at the tales they had embellished night after night. Easily he could explain each one now. Unfortunate Mistress Dyna had less to do with the church roof than the masons who had raised it years before, and Beatrice had contributed no more and no less than the other villagers to the well which was probably poisoned after an animal fell into it and died. And Cybele had been simply lucky and unlucky.

Yet, he could discount all that rational thinking now as he watched Fayette Wychwood flit through the trees like a phantom daring the daylight. In her white dress, with her blond hair drifting out from beneath her straw bonnet and fluttering about her shoulders, she could be, as lief, an angel. Unlikely, for thoughts of her had bedeviled him since he discovered her kneeling in the dirt near the stable.

Her eyes were a cat's green, and she moved with a feline's grace. He smiled at his own roguish thoughts as he wondered if she would be as untamed in a man's arms . . . in his arms.

He was striding through the trees even before the next thought formed in his head. Where had she vanished to? He could understand how the fearful fools around here had marked this family as witches, but he did not believe that nonsense. Following the low stone wall, he edged around a fallen tree to stand beside it.

There, gathering flowers in a basket that was the same shade of green as her mysterious eyes, Miss Wychwood was humming a light tone that had the trill of one of the birds overhead. Around her on the ground, her muslin gown puddled in the moss.

"Good afternoon," he called.

Miss Wychwood flinched, then looked over her shoulder. Her eyes grew wide as her mouth became an "O" of surprise. Slowly rising on the other side of the wall, she said, "My lord, I didn't think—that is, I had not considered—I mean, good afternoon."

"You have some lovely flowers."

"Yes."

"What will you be using them for?"

"Using them for?" Bafflement ruffled her forehead where wisps of hair drifted across the fine line of her brows.

He resisted the temptation to brush those soft strands back and let them slip along his finger. With a laugh, he said, "Many of the folks around here would worry if they saw a Wychwood woman collecting herbs and greens."

"They would have no reason to fret." She drew out one blossom. "These are bound for nothing more exotic than a vase which I will set in the window by the sitting room hearth. Is that a disappointment for you, my lord?"

"Hardly." He bent and plucked another of the small flowers. Holding it out to her, he smiled when he said, "I fear that I am the one who has been disappointing."

"How?"

His eyes were drawn to the graceful motions of her fingers as she slipped the stems back among the others in her basket. "Jeremiah tells me I still owe you the duty of an apology."

"And do you pay your debts swiftly, my lord?"

"Most of them."

"Is that an apology then?"

He sat on the wall between them. "I suspect it may be as close as I shall come to one today." Motioning to the stones beside him, he added, "Do sit here in the shade, Miss Wychwood. You have been out in the sunshine for long enough."

"How do you know that?" She put up her hand to wipe the glistening perspiration from her nape as she sat an arm's length away on the stone wall, her feet securely pressed against the grass on the side opposite his.

He enjoyed watching her slender fingers brush the skin he would like to touch far more eagerly. A gentle scent rose from her, the fragrance of fresh flowers that drew him as surely as if he were a bee. Would her skin be as downy as a flower petal and as sweet as honeysuckle?

Sliding toward her, he put one hand on a stone next to her leg. He smiled when her eyes widened again. She could not rise without bumping into his arm or by put-

ting her feet on his side of the wall. Neither would she
wish to do, so she was his prisoner.

"My lord, I think—'

"You asked how I knew you were out here in the sunshine," he said low enough so only her ears could hear.
"Don't you want an answer?"

"I know I look like a dashed shabrag."

"You look lovely." He did not let her gaze slide away
from his as he twisted his finger in a vagrant lock of her
hair. Something glittered more brightly in her eyes
when he grazed her cheek with the strand, letting his
finger delight in her softness. "I was, you should know,
watching you, Miss Wychwood."

"You were?"

He almost laughed. She was nothing like the ladies
he had met in London. They had learned to trifle with
a man in any of a dozen ways that would leave his heart
pounding and his arms empty. The flutter of a fan, the
arch of a brow, and the light laugh around words that
meant less than nothing-sayings were devices used with
skill throughout the *ton*.

Fayette Wychwood needed none of those, for she possessed an innocence that was more appealing than any
practiced jest. Yet he was not fat-pated enough to believe
she was without wit. She simply was not worldly.

Other worldly, whispered a warning voice in his mind.

"Look," he said, to escape his own uneasy thoughts.
He touched a vine that was threaded through the narrow space between the rocks in the wall.

"Be careful," she warned. "Those briars are painful
if you get them stuck in your finger."

"I will take care, but look at this vine."

She frowned. "It looks like any other that twists
through this copse."

"Save that it has its roots within the soil of Saint's Rest
while its leaves thrive on your side of the wall. Surely

that proves that it is possible to travel from one side of this wall to the other without peril."

"You speak of a plant, my lord, which has no goal during its existence than to grow and bear its fruit. People are quite different."

"Do you believe so?"

At his question, which seemed far too intimate, Fayette wanted to devise an excuse to take her leave, but she could think of no words that would not bring on that hateful blush. She remained perched on the very edge of the stones, her back to the shadow cast by his house across the field.

"What did you do to injure your leg?" The words slipped from her before she could halt them.

He regarded her with amazement. "Didn't Jeremiah fill your head with that flapdoodle?"

"No."

"He usually cannot wait to blither about it."

"About what?"

She was surprised when he looked away. Could he be embarrassed? By his own bravery?

"I chanced to be traveling along Piccadilly when a fire broke out in a home there," he said quietly.

"How many did you save?"

He stared at her. "How do you know?"

" 'Tis not witchcraft, if that is what you are thinking. Just common sense. If you were injured and your brother speaks of it endlessly, it must not be because you hurt yourself scurrying away. You must have done something brave for him to play the windy wallet."

"Two small children were unable to escape from the third floor, and their father was overcome with smoke. Otherwise, he would have done as I did and retrieved them."

"You are making light of something wonderful."

"Something that could have been stupid." He rubbed

his leg absently as he stared beyond her as if looking into the past. "We were fine until the stairs collapsed beneath us. I protected the children from harm, but I broke my leg." His smile returned as he shrugged. "It has healed, and the children are alive. End of the story."

"But you are a hero!"

His smile grew rigid. "You act so astonished, Miss Wychwood. Could it be that you can imagine no one of my line doing something like that?"

Fayette looked away. "If you wish the truth, yes."

"You have had your head filled with pap from the moment of your birth. The St. James family is no better or worse than any other."

"Save to my family."

He grimaced. "I swear that this has gone on long enough!" He swung his legs over the wall and planted his feet on the ground beside hers. "See? Putting my foot on this side of the wall has not brought about Armageddon."

"Not yet."

He chuckled. "I had not thought you to be such a doomsayer."

"It takes nothing more than knowing the menace that has stalked my family in the past."

"I am not the past. Nor are you."

Warmth flowed through her as she lowered her eyes again. How difficult it was to believe that this charming man who was doing all he could to set her at ease could be of the dreadful St. James name.

"I am sorry if I frightened you," he murmured, the words as soft as a caress, "when I came upon you by the stables. You must let me play the host to you again to redress my unthinking words."

"I think not."

"Are you afraid of me?"

She almost said, "Yes." It was the truth, but not for

the reason he was hoaxing her about. She was frightened of the way something sweet melted within her each time he touched her and of how every sane thought was swept from her mind by his smile.

Standing, she replied, "Don't be absurd."

"Then," he said, swinging his legs back over to the far side of the wall, "join me over here."

"I think not," she repeated.

"I think so." Grasping her at the waist, he lifted her over the wall and set her firmly in front of him. His hands tightened again on her waist when she stepped away. With as little ease as he had hoisted her to this side of the wall, he held her in place between his knees.

She gasped, "Release me at once!"

"What is frightening you so?" he asked.

"I should not be here."

"Why not? I invited you. I am the owner of Saint's Rest."

"I should not be here."

Standing, he slid his hands up her arms in a slow caress. She took a step backward. He kept the distance between them the same. Disquiet became dismay as his fingers glided along her shoulder, brushing her bare skin with lightning.

She gasped and turned to climb back over the wall. As she put her foot into a crevice, her boot slipped. She choked back a cry as pain swept up her shin and down her arm. Before she could fall, strong arms enfolded her to an unyielding chest.

"Are you hurt?" he asked.

An absurd question, for she was blind with the anguish that throbbed in her limbs. "Yes!"

"By all that's blue! You are bleeding."

"Am I?" She started to look down, then swayed. No, she could not swoon. Not here. Not in front of Lord St. James.

He muttered something. It was scanty warning before he put his arm beneath her knees and swept her up to his chest. Before she could do more than gasp, he had settled her securely in his arms and was striding across the field. Her eyes widened in horror when she realized he was walking toward the manor house.

"Take me home," she cried.

"Exactly what I had in mind." He continued to climb up the hill.

"No! *My* home!" She tried to wiggle out of his arms.

His chuckle curled through her, leaving a most unexpected longing in its wake. A longing to toss aside caution and lean her head against his shoulder as she let him watch over her. Was she queer in her attic? Of all the men in this world, she should trust this one least.

"Let me go," she ordered with all the dignity she had remaining.

"No."

She struggled to escape again. "My lord, if you don't release me, you may persuade me to do something I regret."

"If you don't stop squirming in my arms, you may persuade me to do something I shall *not* regret."

Fayette stared up at his rakish grin and the fierce fires within his eyes. They left no question of what he meant with his hardly cryptic threat.

She subsided, not knowing what else to do. If she continued to protest, she feared he would do as he threatened. Her heart leaped, washing away the pulse of pain. She *was* a loose screw. To let him hold her like this was crazy, but to imagine his mouth over hers . . . She must be dicked in the nob.

When he shifted her in his arms, the agony gushed up her leg again. She moaned and nodded when he hastily apologized. She could not speak. She could do nothing, save close her eyes and concentrate on something other than that overpowering pain.

Coolness touched her face, and she opened her eyes to discover Lord St. James had carried her inside the manor house. She dampened the chill that ran along her spine. No firstborn Wychwood woman had been within these walls since the signing of the Magna Carta.

In spite of herself, she could not keep from staring. The entry hall was resplendent with sunlight that splashed onto the marble floor from the windows high in the rafters above. Wide doors opened off the hall which was five-sided. Flowers brightened a quartet of rooms, as if the garden had been brought inside. The fifth door opened to a stairwell where the simple oak banister curved up and out of sight.

"Welcome to Saint's Rest," he said softly.

"I should not be here."

"But you are, and . . ." He looked past her as footfalls rushed toward them.

She followed his gaze to meet the bewildered eyes of a brown-haired woman dressed in a simple gown that announced her station as housekeeper. Lord St. James's words confirmed her guess.

"Mrs. Darby," he said, "have some cool compresses brought to clean the dirt from Miss Wychwood's scrapes."

"Wychwood?" The thin woman backed away, her eyes as fearful as if a hell-born hag were looming over her.

Cassidy muttered a curse under his breath when the housekeeper's fingers twisted in the ancient sign against evil. Stories under the covers with his brother had been amusing, but this was madcap. Mrs. Darby was no peagoose, ready to accept as gospel every legend whispered in the village.

"Mrs. Darby, if you please."

At his sharp tone, the housekeeper blinked and nodded like a child waking from a deep slumber. She scurried away, glancing back several times. Even before the door closed to the kitchen, he heard Mrs. Darby call, "You will never in a lifetime guess whom Lord St. James has brought into this house! That Wychwood woman! The firstborn one! God have mercy on our souls."

Fayette must have heard, too, for she stiffened in his arms. Wanting to apologize for the insensitive comments, but not sure how, he wondered, for the first time, what it must have been like growing up here in a family that was rumored to possess all of Satan's secrets. She was doomed to be forever an outcast in her own village.

Carrying her into his book-room, where the myriad eyes of the staff would not be focused upon them as the servants devised a dozen silly reasons to pass by, he set her carefully on the settee. He frowned when he saw the blood staining his sleeve. She must be more than scratched.

"This really is not a good idea," she argued again, but her voice was faint. "Auntie Delphina is capable of patching me up."

"And putting a curse on me to avenge the damage I caused her niece."

She squared her shoulders and raised her chin. "That is not funny."

He smiled. "Good. 'Tis just as I suspected."

"What did you suspect?" she asked, her eyes narrowing with distrust.

"Insulting you works more effectively than burning feathers in order to rescue you from vapors." He pulled up a footstool and sat facing her. "I do despise that odor of burnt feathers even more than *sal volatile.*"

"So do I." Her voice softened again as she leaned back against the cushions.

"Don't swoon on me, or I shall have to insult you and your family again."

"I shall endeavor not to, if you will act like a gentleman."

"A tough bargain." He reached for the hem of her skirt. "And one I cannot, at the moment, keep."

A scream bubbled in Fayette's throat as Lord St. James raised her skirt up her leg. She clamped her lips closed, so it would not escape when he bent to examine the injury her own clumsiness had caused.

"What the deuce!" he exclaimed.

"Is it bad?" She was sure it must be, because fire still danced on her leg.

He gave her no answer as he untied his cravat and dabbed the white linen against the dampness on her skin. When she could not silence her moan, he whispered, "I am sorry, Miss Wychwood."

Or she thought he said that. Darkness gnawed at the edges of the room. She could not fight it and fell into the pit as endless as a nightmare.

"Miss Wychwood . . . Fayette?" A hand tapped Fayette's cheek lightly. "Fayette, can you hear me?"

Fayette turned her face against fabric that smelled of woodsmoke and fresh, autumn air. She did not want to wake from this dream where everything was possible. Somehow, she had escaped from the nightmare, for now she floated as free as a leaf atop a brook.

"Fayette?" The deep voice rumbled beneath her cheek.

She tried to sit, then collapsed back against the hard pillow. Not a pillow, she realized with a start, but Lord St. James's arm.

"My lord," she whispered, as her gaze locked with his, "I should not—"

"You should not call me 'my lord' after you have been slumbering so prettily in my arms." His rakish grin was gentled by the concern drawing lines in his face. Moving to sit on the footstool in front of her, he dabbed at her forehead with the cool cloth. "I collect this is the first time anyone from my family has said such a thing to someone from yours."

"I collect you are wrong. In 1183, Eartha, firstborn daughter of Arthur de Wychwood was set upon by Lord St. James and his brother at the bridge—"

"What the deuce! Do you know the history of every Wychwood woman who has lived since the beginning of time?"

She closed her eyes to relish the coolness against her fevered face. "Not since the beginning of time, but certainly since the first Lord St. James."

"Has there been one Wychwood woman who was not persecuted by my family?"

"Yes."

"How many?"

She opened her eyes and smiled weakly. "Quite a few, but those women were fortunate enough for their Lords St. James to be called away to fight for king and country."

"I fear 'tis your misfortune that the war with France has come to an end."

"Misfortune?"

"Jeremiah was in quite a prime to have us both buy commissions and cross the Channel to give a poke to Boney's boltsprit." He smoothed her hair back from her eyes as he laughed softly. "I was grateful when peace interceded before he persuaded me that was a good idea."

"I doubt he could persuade you to do anything you chose not to. I would think, as lief, you would be the one to influence him."

His brow arched. "I have far less sway over my brother than I would like."

"Mayhap because he wishes to live the life of a decent gentleman. Venetia has said . . ."

"Go on. This could be most amusing."

She shook her head, then wished she had not. The rumble aching in her leg and along her arm detonated within her skull.

"Make haste slowly, Fayette." He dabbed her forehead with the cool cloth again. "Your wounds, although not serious, shall be bothersome for a few days, I suspect." The cloth edged along her cheek in a gentle caress that was anything but cool. "I suspect, as well, that Venetia Tanner is deeply involved in whatever puts that guilty expression on your face whenever her or Jeremiah's name is mentioned."

"She is my bosom-bow. I should not prattle about her."

"She would gladly prattle about you." He grinned. "And she has, for many ears in London are privy to the dark tales that have haunted this shire since the beginning of memory."

"Venetia would not hurt—" At his laugh, she began again. "Venetia would not intentionally hurt a friend."

"But she would be glad to gather what prestige she might gain among the *ton* when she claims that she has the *amitié* of an authentic, cauldron-stirring witch."

"I do not stir a cauldron!" Leaning back against the cushions, she added, "Just the pots in the kitchen."

"So you are only an apprentice witch?"

"You are being absurd!"

"I—" He stood as quiet footsteps came toward the book-room.

Fayette bit her lower lip as a gray-haired woman entered the room, followed by a young maid who was carrying a basin. The older woman set a roll of bandaging on a table by the settee. Backing away hastily, she herded the maid before her out the door.

"Pay them no mind," Cassidy said, irritation honing his voice.

"I don't. I expected nothing less."

He sat on the stool in front of her again. "You have more forbearance for fools than I."

"I have become accustomed to the stares and the way every word I speak is likely to be misconstrued."

"Do you mind?" He touched the torn hem of her gown.

Fayette gasped, "You are going to bandage my leg?"

"Would you expect Mrs. Darby to? She is so frightened, she would not dare to come close to you."

"But Auntie Delphina—"

"Is not here." He dipped one end of the bandaging into the basin. Meeting her eyes evenly, he said, "This should be tended to without delay."

"All right." Even to her own ears, her voice sounded rather faint.

"Trust me, Fayette." He laughed without mirth. "I suspect I am not the first of my family to say that to one of your ancestors."

"I suspect you are right." She winced as he dabbed the lint against her skin.

"And I further suspect you believe it no more than they did."

Tears filled her eyes, but she refused to let them fall. He made quick work of the task, tying a strip of the material around her shin. As he was smoothing her gown modestly back into place, a laugh came from the doorway.

Fayette gasped as Cassidy set himself on his feet with a muttered oath aimed at his brother. Jeremiah St. James leaned one shoulder nonchalantly against the door frame and crossed his arms over his chest. Looking from one brother to the other, she was astonished anew how alike and how unlike they were. While Cassidy's smile could be infuriating, she never had seen it possess the icy hauteur in his brother's.

"Have you forgotten your manners, brother?" Cassidy asked as he tossed the last bit of bandaging onto the table next to the basin.

"I knocked."

"Did you?"

Jeremiah chuckled. "You seemed intent on your task which seems to have been focused on Miss Wychwood's lower limbs. I applaud your good taste, Cassidy."

Fayette tried to sit straighter, readying a retort that would burn his ears for days. Even though she was reclining on the settee in this very private book-room with Cassidy leaning over her, nothing untoward had happened.

Cassidy put his hand gently on her shoulder. His light stroke, which she guessed was meant to be consoling, sent pleasure surging through her. If he had touched her like this before his brother arrived . . .

She was saved from the enchantment of her own fantasies when Cassidy said in the coldest voice she had ever heard, "Do not insult Fayette by jumping to erroneous conclusions. I was doing no more than what any good neighbor should. She scraped her leg on a stone on the wall separating our lands, and I tended to her injury. Do not add to her wounds by spouting bangers like a cabbage-head."

"I meant the lady no harm. However, it seems, Cassidy, you are in the unenviable situation of needing to make amends to Miss Wychwood again." Jeremiah flashed a much warmer smile at her. "I can think of but one way to atone for your misdeeds."

"Cassidy—I mean, Lord St. James owes me no obligation," she hurried to say as she carefully pushed her skirt farther down over her ankles.

"Nonsense." Jeremiah refocused his smile on his brother. "You have done this beautiful, young woman a grievous wrong, Cassidy. You must right it by granting me leave to invite her and her dear friend Miss Tanner to dinner Saturday evening."

"Saturday evening?" she asked. "That is—"

"Impossible. I agree." Cassidy's laugh was lean and cold. "Do you intend it to be just the four of us? Such a coze would be the *on dits* for weeks to come."

"I would do nothing to besmirch the reputation of Miss Wychwood and Miss Tanner."

"No?" He walked to where his brother had folded his arms on the back of a wing chair. "Can it be that you have something in mind other than a *tête-à-tête-à-tête-à-tête?*"

"Why not a rout? Things have been so quiet since the end of the Little Season. I tire of wandering about the meadows, looking for game."

"So you would as lief do your hunting here?" asked Cassidy.

"Why not? A small gathering Saturday evening will put an end to the blue devils plaguing all of us."

Fayette raised her voice slightly. "I cannot attend."

She was ignored as Cassidy scowled at his brother and asked, "How long have you been scheming this?"

"When I saw Miss Tanner and Miss Wychwood looking so lovely—" He flashed Fayette a generous smile. "—and so lonely, inspiration seized me. I have the guest list all planned, and, if the weather is fine Saturday evening, we can use the terrace for the final time this year before the cold drives us back inside."

"I cannot attend," Fayette said a bit louder.

Cassidy held out his hand to his brother who slapped a piece of paper on it. He scanned what she guessed was the guest list before saying, "With half the shire invited, I cannot accuse you, Jeremiah, of arranging this so you might enjoy a forbidden tryst with Miss Tanner."

"Or you with Miss Wychwood." He winked boldly at her.

"Watch your tongue!" Cassidy snapped.

"Do you think she might steal it from me with an enchantment? Make me as mute as a stump?"

"It might not be such a bad idea."

"I cannot attend," Fayette fairly shouted.

The two brothers turned to look at her, shock on their faces.

Folding her hands primly in her lap, she said, "If you will cease your brangle long enough to listen to me, I can tell you that you are wasting your time arguing about inviting me. I cannot attend dinner Saturday evening."

"And why, pray tell, not?" Jeremiah's smile fled from his face, shocking her anew. Until this afternoon, she had not guessed his easygoing manner covered this haughtiness when she dared to countermand his plans.

She swallowed roughly. "It is All Hallows' Eve."

"Then you must come and do some magic for us." Jeremiah wafted his hand through the air. "A spell or two to amaze and enthrall us."

"I am not a stage magician or a conjurer who travels about the countryside performing at fairs."

"All the better." He turned to his brother. "Think of the fun we can have. Our gathering will be spoken of for years to come. How many hosts can claim to have a real witch among their guests?"

"Jeremiah, enough!" Cassidy ordered.

He laughed and clapped his brother on the shoulder. "I understand."

"You understand what?"

"You want to keep her magic to yourself." With another chuckle, he walked to the door. He added, as he drew the door closed behind him, "A wise decision."

Cassidy grumbled something under his breath, and Fayette decided it would be wise not to ask him to repeat it. Going to the door, he opened it.

He faced her and smiled wryly. "Since you have been

regaling me with the misdeeds of my ancestors through the centuries, I cannot help but wonder if someone in your family put on a curse on mine."

"A curse?"

"Jeremiah. He is enough to try a saint's patience, and, in spite of my name, I am no saint."

"Auntie Delphina refused to teach me any black magic. She said knowing such things can only bring wickedness back on me."

"I meant that as a jest." His brow furrowed as he frowned. "Do you mean you really believe you can do magic?"

"Yes."

He laughed, shaking his head. "Mayhap you are as moonstruck as I've heard Wychwood women are."

Fayette recoiled. How dare he mock her! The small charms and incantations had served her family well. Knowing what plants would ease pain and which would help heal had saved many lives.

Coolly, she said, "I thank you for tending to the results of my clumsiness."

"Clumsy? You?" He put his hand on the back of the settee, so close to her shoulder that she could sense the heat of his flesh. Leaning toward her, he murmured, "I wasn't plying you with out-and-outers when I said earlier that I was watching you in the greenwood. You were as graceful as a swan upon a pond."

She should not let him woo her with his nothing-sayings. She should shove him aside and demand that he have her shown to the door. But she did not want to lose a moment of the warm caress of his gaze or the furtive touch of his fingertips against her nape. Her breath seared her chest, for she did not dare release it as he bent even nearer.

She could not draw her gaze from his lips as he whispered, "Do join us at this impromptu assembly."

"I appreciate the generosity of your invitation," she said, lowering her eyes, "but I cannot attend on Saturday."

"You can on Friday evening."

"Jeremiah said—"

"As master of Saint's Rest, I have the luxury of upsetting my brother's plans whenever I wish." He took her hand as she tried to stand. "Fayette, be careful. You should sit a while longer."

"Mama shall be worrying about me. I must go home." Her words came with the speed of a blizzard's blast. She must flee from here before she let herself get sucked into the enchantment conjured up by her own yearning for his touch.

"I think you should remain here. Mrs. Darby is preparing a room for you."

"Mama would—"

"Your mother is welcome here, too."

Her laugh sounded brittle. "She would as lief sit down to dinner with the devil."

"Then I shall send her a message that you are remaining here."

She shook her head, then wondered if her brain had become loose, for her eyes refused to focus. Forcing what remained of her waning strength into her voice, she said, "I must go home."

"You need not worry about anything untoward happening here."

Although she knew she was being caper-witted, she did not draw away when he put his finger beneath her chin. She tipped her head back to look up into his eyes which were as blue and as infinite as a cloudless autumn sky. Letting herself become lost in them, she did not move when they came closer. She had heard of magicians who could put a subject in a trance simply with a deep gaze. Mayhap he had cast a spell over her.

She pulled away with a soft cry. Hobbling to the door, she paused only when he called her name. She looked back to see him by the settee.

"I will expect you here by nine on Friday evening," he said. Crossing the room, he put his finger to her lips as she was about to speak. "Do not disappoint me by giving me some tale of why you must refuse this invitation, Fayette." He raised her hand to brush it with a swift kiss that sent heated shivers fluttering through her. "I do not want to be disappointed."

"I cannot promise I will be there."

"Promise me you will try." His fingers splayed across her cheek, and he tilted her face toward him, leaving no more than a breath's breadth between them.

As she was lost once more in his mesmerizing eyes, she nodded, surrendering to the temptation of his touch. When his lips tilted in a satisfied smile, she no longer cared that she might be damning herself as thoroughly as her ancestors had.

Fayette's hopes that she might escape notice when she entered the cottage were dashed when her great-aunt called from the sitting room, "What happened to you?" Auntie Delphina shook her head with a sad smile. "I need not ask, now that Lord St. James has returned."

"This was not his doing. I was clumsy when I was trying to climb back over the stone wall. I—" She put her hands to her lips.

Auntie Delphina frowned as she came out into the hall. "I warned you not to go onto the lands of Saint's Rest."

"I had not intended to. Lord St. James approached me, and, while we were speaking—"

"I do not want to hear all the details of your tryst."

"Auntie!"

Her great-aunt sighed. "Forgive me, child. I fear for you when I think of the wickedness that has stained this earth for so many centuries." Brushing Fayette's hair back from her eyes, she whispered, "I want to keep that horror from touching you."

"Cassidy is not evil."

"You address him as Cassidy?" She rubbed her chin. "This is growing far more complicated than I had guessed."

Fayette sat on the bench at the foot of the stairs. "Auntie, he asked me to call him that. How could I refuse in the wake of his kindness?"

"What kindness? Seducing you?"

"Auntie! He did no more than oversee the bandaging of my leg." That was almost the truth, for she did not want to own to Auntie Delphina that she had been ready to throw her arms around Cassidy when they stood by the door to his book-room.

"I hope so."

"Auntie, just because his name is Lord St. James, that does not mean he is the devil personified."

"Only to the firstborn daughter of the Wychwood name."

Fayette sighed. "I know. Can we speak of something else?" She leaned forward and brushed dirt from her great-aunt's apron. "Have you been working in the garden all afternoon? What harvest can there be left?"

"Some things need time to grow, child." Auntie Delphina patted her on the head. "As you have, but it appears that you have blossomed from a child into a woman. All the more reason you should fear Lord St. James."

"Don't even speak that name in this house!" cried Mama, rushing out of the kitchen at the back of the house. "Oh, my dear Fayette, what happened to you? Did that horrible man do something to you?"

Rising awkwardly, because her leg was stiff, Fayette smiled. "Mama, do not be absurd. I bumped my leg against one of the stones in the wall. It is nothing." She glanced at Auntie Delphina. Would her great-aunt blurt out the truth?

"Calm yourself," Auntie Delphina said to Mama. "She is just scratched."

"You must go directly to bed and stay there," Mama ordered. "A few day's rest will heal that."

"Impossible," Fayette said at the same time as Auntie Delphina.

"What do you mean?"

"All Hallows' Eve is nearly upon us," Auntie Delphina said. "She must not cower in her bed when she should be celebrating." A smile curled across her lips. "And, if I am not mistaken, Fayette already has plans of her own for the evening before that."

Fayette wanted to ask her great-aunt how she could perceive the truth with such ease, but she knew Auntie Delphina would only give her that secretive smile and tell her that some skills would become hers only with the passage of the years. Sitting on the bench once more, she steeled herself for Mama's next question.

"What plans?" Mama asked.

Wanting to demur, but unwilling to speak a clanker to her mother, Fayette said, "Lord St. James is having a gathering that evening."

"You cannot be thinking of going there." Mama whirled to Auntie Delphina. "Tell her she is mad!"

"She knows."

Mama turned back to Fayette. "Child, to go there endangers you in ways you cannot, in your innocence, guess. Those men are our enemies. They have advanced themselves upon the spilled blood of our family." She hid her face in her hands. "Oh, dear God, why did I ever agree to come back here after your father's death?"

As Fayette comforted her mother, she waited for Auntie Delphina to speak. Her great-aunt remained oddly silent. That silence disturbed her more than anything else today.

A knock on the door interrupted Auntie Delphina, who was reading aloud from Fayette's favorite novel. "See who it might be, child. Mrs. Jennings is busy in the kitchen."

Fayette rose, delighted that her leg no longer stabbed with pain on each step. When she opened the door, she gasped, "Cassidy, what are you doing here?"

"You promised me you would come to our gathering." He doffed his beaver hat. The lamplight glittered on his ebony hair and the brilliant white of his cravat beneath his navy velvet coat. Silver breeches were as bright as the buckles on his shoes.

"But it is tomorrow evening."

"Didn't you receive my message about the change in plans?"

"No, my lord, she did not." Mama's voice was sterner than Fayette had ever heard. Putting her hand on Fayette's arm, she stepped only a single pace into the hall. "*I* intercepted it. Fayette will not be joining you at Saint's Rest this evening or any other. We bid you good evening and good-bye, my lord."

She stared at her mother. She never had heard Mama speak with such authority. Looking back at Cassidy, she saw the amazement in his eyes darkening into vexation.

When he bowed toward them and turned to leave, he paused. "Madam, do not begrudge me a moment to speak with Fayette before I take my leave." His voice was as cool as the night breeze swirling into the hall.

Before Mama could answer, Auntie Delphina came out of the sitting room and leaned on her cane. "You may speak with her on the front step." Auntie Delphina stared at Cassidy, but he did not quail before her as Fayette's few suitors from the village had before they fled, never to return.

Dipping his head again, he said, "I am grateful for your indulgence."

"You shall indulge in nothing more than speaking with my grand-niece." She added to Fayette, "Leave the door ajar. Your mother and I shall be here by the stairs."

Fayette nodded as she glanced from Auntie Delphina's out-thrust chin to the fear bleaching Mama's face and then to Cassidy's stern frown. When he offered his arm, she hesitated. His dark brow quirked like a bird's wing caught in an updraft, and a hint of a smile tugged at his lips. A most challenging smile, which dared her to choose between the canons of propriety and her trepidation.

She heard Mama's soft intake of breath when she let Cassidy draw her fingers within his arm. As he put his hand over hers, she could not pull her gaze from his. She wanted to be beside him like this, to be spellbound by the possibility that she could remain here, his touch lighting her soul.

The enchantment vanished when, as soon as she had stepped out into the cold, he pulled her toward the grand carriage waiting on the road linking her home with his. He swung her up onto the seat beneath the dim lantern.

"Are you mad?" she cried as he climbed in beside her. "Auntie Delphina said no farther than the front step." She reached for the door.

He captured her hand and gently drew it back to fold her fingers between his. "Fayette . . ."

"Release me at once!"

"Fayette, I must . . ."

"You must release me without delay." She tried to tug away. "I shall scream. I vow I shall!"

As she opened her mouth, his glove covered it. He bent close to her, his voice as deep and low as the night's shadows. "Why are you acting like an irritating child when I called to quell my fear that you still suffered from your injuries?"

She tried to give him a back-answer, but only mumbles reached her ears.

"I have seen you are walking well," he continued, "and your mother's explanation tells me why you have not joined us at Saint's Rest." He swore under his breath. "Confound it, Fayette! This is a damnable way to have a conversation."

When he slowly drew his hand away, she snapped, "How dare you treat me like this! I have nothing to say to you."

"Good, because . . ." His arms swept around her.

She opened her mouth to protest, but his lips covered hers. Tender, deepening as he pressed her against the back of the velvet seat, his kiss sought to waken every pleasure within her. His fingers splayed across her shoulders, holding her so close she brushed against his hard chest with every ragged breath. Letting her fingers sweep up through the ebony satin of his hair, she moaned softly when his mouth blazed sweet fire along her neck.

He did not release her as he whispered against her ear, "I want you to stop whatever you are doing to make Jeremiah so dashed moony."

Fayette had not expected him to say something like this in the wake of the luscious ecstasy. Drawing back, she asked, "Me? I am doing nothing."

"Now."

She submerged the shudder that cut across her shoulders as if the wind had become winter cold. Never had she met anyone—other than Auntie Delphina—who could see the truth so clearly. Every attempt she made to hide the truth seemed to work in the reverse and enable him to tear down another layer of her façade to reveal the truth no one must know.

"Fayette, my brother is not himself." His eyes hardened. "He longs to spend every minute with Miss Tanner. Even with a dozen other women in the room, he cannot keep away from her. Why?"

"Mayhap he has a *tendre* for her."

"Unlikely. My brother is a prime rake. Jeremiah is as constant in his affections as a cat on the prowl. He will promise your friend a place in every crevice of his heart until it takes its next beat. If all goes as it has in the past, he will steal your friend's heart, then break it."

"It shan't be as it was in the past."

"How can you be so certain?" He laughed sharply. "Do not tell me that you believe all those old tales of hocus-pocus?"

"It is not just hocus-pocus."

He grasped her shoulders and leaned his face, which was as taut as the moment they had met, close to hers. "I do not care a farthing if you believe it is magic or not, but you must persuade Miss Tanner to listen to sense. I will not stand by and watch Jeremiah break another heart."

"Although there is no need, for the charm will not work unless both hearts desire it, I will speak with Venetia."

"Now?" He glanced toward the manor house.

Fayette followed his gaze. For so long, the house had been almost abandoned on its lonely hill. Now it was alight, an earthbound star twinkling through the trees. His fingers against her cheek brought her back to stare up at the fiery emotions glittering in his eyes. Every story she had heard about the wicked Lords St. James flew through her head in a macabre quadrille. She dismissed them all as he cupped her chin in his palm.

"I cannot," she said. "I told Mama I would not go to Saint's Rest again."

"What frightens you?" His finger slid up her cheek to tilt her mouth beneath his. "Does this frighten you?"

His lips seared that forbidden pleasure into hers. For a moment, she let the rapture melt her to him. She gripped the front of his coat when he brazenly sought deep within her mouth, snatching away her breath. His laugh warmed her face as he sparked kisses across her cheek.

"No!" she gasped as he began to recline her back on the seat. "Release me, or—"

"Or what? Will you turn me into a toad?"

"No need! You have the demeanor of one already!" She shoved herself out of his arms, blinking back tears. She had shrugged others' cruel comments off as ignorance, but, somehow, she had dared to believe Cassidy St. James would be different. She had hoped that he would overcome his prejudice and accept this unique part of her. What an air-dreamer she had been! He was the same as the rest of his family.

A pang coursed up her leg when she jumped out of the carriage. She slammed the door shut.

"Fayette!" he called.

She ran into the cottage, not slowing until she reached her bedchamber under the eaves. Dropping to sit on the stool by the window, she could not keep from watching the carriage drive away. Tears, thick and hot, flowed down her cheeks.

When Auntie Delphina came into the room, Fayette threw her arms around her great-aunt and sobbed.

"Hush, child. It will come to rights."

"How can it?" she gulped. "How can it, when I believe I love him?"

"Love him? Lord St. James?"

She nodded as she looked out the window at the lights glowing from Saint's Rest. "I fear nothing can save me now from my own flummery."

"Don't fret, child. I shall deal with it."

"Auntie Delphina, no!"

Her great-aunt smiled. "Trust me, child. I know just what to do." She hobbled out of the room, leaving Fayette to wonder what catastrophe she had called down upon them now.

Fayette rushed homeward in the early twilight. Tonight was All Hallows' Eve, and she would not risk being abroad and meeting a group of villagers bent on mischief.

Her steps faltered when she saw something lying in the middle of the narrow path. Had someone lost a cloak? Had Cassidy? She fought her feet which yearned to rush forward, so she could gather the material up in her arms. To touch something that was his . . . She scowled. She was being as witless as Venetia.

Her bosom-bow refused to destroy the flower which she was tending with such affection. Even when Fayette recounted what Cassidy had told her, Venetia would not listen.

Fayette stopped in midstep as she stared at what she had thought was no more than a lost cloak. "Auntie Delphina!"

She ran and knelt next to her great-aunt who was prone on the ground, her eyes closed, her breathing labored. Lifting Auntie Delphina's head to lie upon her lap, Fayette looked in both directions along the road. How could it be so empty on All Hallows' Eve? Where were the youngsters who should be enjoying mischief tonight? Had all of them set aside the old traditions to save their mischief for celebrating Guy Fawkes's Day later in the week?

Someone help me! Please.

As the twilight vanished into darkness, she did not dare move. Auntie Delphina's eyes remained shut, and Fayette feared her great-aunt would die if she were left alone while Fayette went to get the cart. This was all her doing. Auntie Delphina must have been out collecting whatever she needed to put a curse on Cassidy. Then she had taken ill here.

Someone help me! Please.

Footsteps struck the stones along the road. Hope billowed within her. "Can you help?" she cried, praying no knight of the pad was out looking for someone to rob.

"Fayette?"

"Here!" she cried, her heart pounding as she heard Cassidy's voice. "Over here!"

Out of the darkness, he stepped, his cloak swirling about him like a demon's wings. He knelt beside her. "What happened?"

"Auntie Delphina has taken ill." Her voice broke. "I fear she is going to die."

"Come." He stood just as a dray creaked around the corner and into the pool of moonlight. "Let's take her back to Saint's Rest."

"I cannot take her there."

"You must. The doctor should be waiting there by now."

"Doctor?" she asked, astonished, as a trio of burly men brought armfuls of blankets and began to wrap Auntie Delphina in them. "How did you know?"

"You told me."

"Me?" She stared at him. "But that is impossible!"

"Is it?" When she started to ask another question, he

put his hand on her shoulder. "First, let us see to your great-aunt. Explanations can come later."

Fayette struggled to stifle her curiosity as Auntie Delphina was taken to Saint's Rest and into a bedchamber that was nearly the size of the ground floor of the cottage. The doctor ordered her put to bed while he examined her. Going to sit in the outer chamber, Fayette blinked back tears. This was all her doing.

"Can I get you a glass of something to calm you?" Cassidy asked.

Before she could answer, the door reopened. A maid, who was as thin as an anatomy, motioned to Cassidy. Fayette came to her feet and wrung her hands while the maid spoke softly to him.

"What is it?" she whispered when Cassidy faced her. "Is she—is she—?"

"She wants to see you, Fayette."

"How can I go to her? She warned me if I came onto St. James's land again, my life would be changed forever. I never guessed it would be because I would lose her. Why didn't I listen to her?"

He shook her gently. "Save your lamentations for later, Fayette. If she is so ill that she might die, you cannot delay. You must go and listen to her *now.*"

Drawing away, she turned to stare at the door. She reached for the latch, then pulled back. "I can't."

"You must." He took her hand and placed it on the latch. "If you wish, I will go in with you."

"You will?" She looked up to see compassion in his expressive eyes, and she yearned to draw his arms around her. She needed his strength, and she wanted his warmth to fight back the cold fear within her.

"For centuries, Fayette, your family and mine have been at odds, tearing each other apart. Let it stop here." He drew her hand up to lift the latch.

The door swung open. She tried to take a deep

breath, but nothing could ease the cramp as bands of fear tightened around her chest.

Fayette paid no attention to the lovely furnishings and the grand, black marble hearth as she raced to the high bed where Auntie Delphina was propped against a mound of pillows. She looked as delicate as a rose petal.

Auntie Delphina slowly opened her eyes. "Fayette?"

"Yes, Auntie Delphina, I am here."

"I know." She closed her eyes and nodded. "You have brought one of them with you. How could you bring one of them here?"

"He lives here, Auntie Delphina. This is Saint's Rest."

Her mouth twisted. "You brought me here on All Hallows' Eve?" Her laugh was weak. "What irony! But why did you bring him in here to spread his evil upon me at my last breaths?"

"Cassidy wishes to see how you are, too." Fayette glanced at him, but he was talking intently with the doctor.

"Do not lie to me, child." She smiled, although her eyes remained closed. "Did you know I gave you your name?"

"No."

"Fayette. Little one who is fey. Little fairy child. Someday, it may be your turn to name the next Wychwood firstborn daughter."

"I am afraid not. I shall be the last."

"True." She scowled at Cassidy who took Fayette's hand as he came to stand by the bed. "My lord, I thanked God every day that your grandfather and his son chose to come here only a few days each year. I never guessed that you would be the one to destroy me as all the lords have destroyed all the firstborn daughters of my family. What misfortune that I, who can see the future of those about me, could not see my own!" She moaned so loudly the sound echoed off the walls. "How proud I was that I had escaped the curse! But now I shall pay the price for the knowledge that has been my legacy."

"Auntie Delphina—" Fayette's other hand was grasped by Auntie Delphina's in a grip that was amazingly strong.

"Heed me well, my fey child, for my final words of wisdom must reach your ears before I escape from my last torment at the hands of those who curse us."

"Miss Wychwood?" asked Cassidy quietly.

Auntie Delphina paid him no more attention than she had Fayette. "You know the spells of the heart and how to discern the truth of the emotions hidden within the souls of those around you."

"Miss Wychwood?" Cassidy asked.

Fayette motioned him to silence. How dare he intrude on what might be Auntie Delphina's final words to her!

Her aunt continued as if there had been no interruption, "Here, to the lair of the devil himself, you have been tempted. This man is the spawn of evil. Promise me that—"

"Miss Wychwood," he said in the same calm tone.

"Hush!" Fayette ordered.

He grimaced. "Will you listen to me?"

"Only a cabbage-head heeds the word of the old gentleman in black," intoned Auntie Delphina. "Promise me, Fayette." She coughed weakly.

"Promise you what?"

"Promise me, so I might hear with my last heartbeat, that you will never again—"

"Miss Wychwood," Cassidy interjected again, "I really dislike having to put a damper on your death scene, but—"

"Cassidy!" Fayette gasped. "How can you say such a thing?"

He folded his arms over his chest. "Miss Wychwood, the doctor assures me that you shall recover."

"I shall?" Amazement filled her eyes.

Cassidy smiled at Fayette who stared at him in disbelief. "I am afraid so."

"Why should I trust you? I may be dying at this very moment." Auntie Delphina's strong tone belied her words.

"You may be," he returned in the same even tone. "However, the doctor believes otherwise." He leaned toward the bed, resting his hands on the coverlet. "If you thought to extract a deathbed promise from Fayette that she would never see me again, you are a bit premature."

Auntie Delphina flashed him a frown. "Now, see here, young man—"

"No, you see here." He put his hand on the headboard. "I know you would do anything to prevent Fayette from seeing me again, but you shall need to devise another method."

"There are ways."

Fayette gasped, "No, Auntie Delphina! Do not even speak of such evil."

Cassidy took her hands in his and drew her away from the bed. "It is time to put the evil behind us. Hatred has bound our families together for too many generations in its evil. It is time to put it aside, and let love in."

"Love?" she whispered.

"I am not like my brother," he murmured as he tipped her chin up with the crook of his finger. "When I choose to invite a woman within my heart, I shall not expel her as soon as another diamond of birth chances my way."

"I know."

"You do know, don't you?" His fingertip swept up along her cheek. "Is that the charm the Wychwood women possess? The skill to see the truth that others refuse to acknowledge?"

She looked back at her great-aunt, who was wearing a wide smile and making motions as if digging in the dirt and planting a flower. Too late, she understood what she should have from the beginning. This must have been what Auntie Delphina had meant when she said Fayette's life would never be the same if she came back to Saint's Rest. Her great-aunt had kept every possible *beau* from returning to their cottage . . . until Cassidy. Auntie Delphina must have used the same spell Fayette had given Venetia to bring love to a distant heart and had arranged the whole of this on All Hallows' Eve to bring Fayette back to the man she loved.

Not sure whether to laugh or fly up into the boughs at her aunt's manipulations, she turned back to Cassidy. Gazing up at him, she whispered, "I only know what Auntie Delphina taught me. It has less to do with magic than understanding the nature of plants and animals."

"And of people." His arm slid around her waist, bringing her closer. As her fingers boldly touched his chest, he brushed his lips against her cheek. He smiled as her breath burst from her in delight. Bending to tease her other cheek with a heated kiss, he murmured, "And of my heart."

"Your heart?" Her voice was as faint as a zephyr at dawn.

"I want you within my heart, Fayette, for I love you as I believe I have from the moment I saw you digging in the dirt."

"For my magic, which you discount."

"Oh, I believe in it now. Even if I had not seen its effect upon Jeremiah who is planning to ask Venetia to wed him tonight."

"Oh, how wondrous!"

"Don't you believe in your own magic?"

"I was not quite sure."

He pushed a vagrant strand of hair back from her

face. "When your heart spoke to mine tonight, letting me know how you needed me—"

"You heard that?"

He smiled as secretively as Auntie Delphina. "When I heard your voice within my heart, I knew I was simply denying your special magic that held me spellbound from the first."

"I love you," she whispered, although she wanted to shout the words from the top of Saint's Rest.

He drew her mouth toward his. "Now it's time for me to work a little magic of my own."

The Soul of Indiscretion

Karla Hocker

As a jewel of gold is in a swine's snout,
so is a fair woman which is without discretion.

Proverbs xi, 22.

One

"Amanda, I love you."

Philip's voice, still husky from their shared passion, was a warm caress.

"And I love you." Amanda closed her eyes to stem the tears that surfaced all too easily these days. "I love you with all my heart."

"Why, then, won't you look at me?"

She did not need to open her eyes to see him . . . candlelight dancing on silver threads in unruly dark hair, the shadowed face with its strong, lean jaw. The nose, slightly crooked since it had been broken in a boyhood fistfight at Eton. The mouth that could kiss away her doubts and send her spirits soaring, or could tighten in disapproval and plummet her into despair. His body, all muscle and sinew, covering and warming her; his heartbeat against her breast, his breath on her skin. No, she did not need to open her eyes.

"Amanda." A spatter of kisses along her shoulder, her neck, the curve of her mouth, "Look at me. Surely, after all these years—ten years, my love—you won't revert to bridal shyness?"

Slowly, she opened her eyes. His gaze was tender, and he was smiling—a rare occurrence this past twelve-month or more.

She touched his mouth, the treasured smile. "Philip,

why can we not be like this in London? Loving . . . tender. Why must we always be at odds?"

His smile faded. The sudden stillness in the chamber amplified the howl of a fierce October gale, the pounding of the North Sea against the cliffs beneath their windows.

Philip rolled to the edge of the bed, and immediately Amanda felt cold. Clutching the down cover, she sat up and watched him thrust his arms into the sleeves of his dressing gown. He tied the sash with forceful, jerky tugs.

His voice, however, was smooth. The rector's voice. The politician's voice. "My dear Amanda, this is hardly a propitious moment."

"But it is why you brought me here, is it not? To discuss our differences."

"Discussion, I have learned to my sorrow, will not mend matters."

"Pray, Philip, don't—"

"Don't what?"

"Don't speak to me in that tone . . . as if I were one of the unfortunate girls in Magdalen Home. And if we haven't come here for privacy and an opportunity of uninterrupted discourse, what, then, are we doing on this godforsaken island? You know I have no liking for the sea. Or the northern clime. Or solitude."

"I have cautioned you against exaggeration, Amanda." He picked her nightgown off the floor and handed it to her. "In the first place, Darring Court is hardly a solitary dwelling on the island. Second, it is news to me that God forsook Northumberland or any of the isles. And third, as you should know, my visit here is mandatory."

"Your grandfather's will. I *do* know, Philip. But must you quibble?" She pulled the flannel gown over her head. "It is no wonder we cannot have a conversation. Whatever I say, you listen only for what you consider flaws in my speech and start lecturing me, and I lose heart and want only to keep my thoughts to myself."

"I wish that were the case when you have discourse with my friends."

Her insides knotted. She, who chattered like a magpie with a perfect stranger, or debated Philip's clerical and political friends without a qualm, could be struck mute when confronted by the husband she loved so dearly. Thus it happened more and more frequently since Philip had resigned from his country parish to pursue a new vocation in London.

"You know I am correct," he said. "Speech before thought is your besetting fault." He studied her in silence, his gaze turning tender once more. "But I would not have chosen this moment to raise a subject that must be painful to us both."

"No, indeed. And I already regret having spoken. I wish . . . I wish I had your sense of timing. *You* would not have spoiled our lovemaking thus."

He sat on the edge of the bed, leaned toward her, his hands cradling her face. "I missed you, Amanda. It has been far too long. My fault, I know. I have been gone so much, and—"

"And we quarrel," she finished for him.

Tears pricked her eyes. She blinked them away. How detestable that she was turning into a watering pot. Her mother used to cry with little or no provocation, and nothing had been more tiresome.

"I missed you, too, Philip."

"Let us make a pact. For four days, we'll forget everything that is troublesome. Four days and nights, we shan't discuss anything unpleasant, won't even think of it. We shall strive only to recapture the companionship and joy of our early years."

"How deliciously tempting!"

"We're agreed, then? No mention of anything problematic?"

"Oh, yes! It sounds delightful. But, four days, Philip? Do we not have another day, a fifth day and night, before we return to town?"

He did not answer immediately but moved his fingers in a gentle caress behind her ears and along her neck. "That last day, my love, we must be serious. I shall tell you what must be done to eradicate your unfortunate habit."

"Philip!" The reproach spilled forth as she expelled the breath she hadn't realized she'd held. "As if I could be like you! Putting that fifth day from my mind and not giving it a thought until it arrives. How can you be so . . . so ruthless!"

He rose, looking down at her. "Ruthless. A strange accusation from the woman who used to praise my orderly mind."

"I praised it in the man who said he loved my liveliness. My forthrightness." She slid from the bed, shivering as one foot missed the rug and landed on cold floorboards. "Philip, I have thought of nothing but our differences and the talk we must have. For two long, miserable days, shut in that drafty, bouncing carriage—while you, I might point out, rode and generally pleased yourself!"

"Did you wish to ride a part of the way?" With the candle from the night table, he lit the candles on the dresser. "You should have told me."

"Was I given the opportunity? Philip, are there no lamps in this house? Candles are so old-fashioned and dim."

"My grandfather did not like the smell of lamps."

"Neither do I. But they are brighter." Without pause, she switched back to the previous topic. "How could I tell you that I wished to ride? You did not even stop to ask if I wished to accompany you to Darring Court. You left orders for the maid to pack, then disappeared until the carriage was at the door."

"There was much to be done before our departure." Philip looked tired. "After all, you had just called Lord Knarsdale a miser and a hypocrite."

"I did not."

"Amanda, I heard you."

"If you heard, you must know I did not mention anything like miser or hypocrite."

"Now, who is quibbling over words?"

Once more the howl of the October gale, the sea pounding against the cliffs, sounded unnaturally loud.

And it was cold in the room, the fire in the hearth barely aglow and only a few logs remaining in the basket. Amanda stepped into fleecy slippers and flung a thick tartan shawl around her shoulders.

She looked at her husband. "I don't deny that Lord Knarsdale contributes to various charities. But he doesn't hesitate to use his cane if some unfortunate soul dares accost him in the street. He *is* a hypocrite! And I wish I had, indeed, called him that to his face."

"And I wish you would think before you speak. Knarsdale is the most open-handed philanthropist in the country. He is a powerful and influential voice in Parliament. He is the man who can get me elected to the House of Commons."

"He can also make you compromise your values."

Philip's face was at its most expressionless as he leaned against the dresser, arms crossed uncompromisingly against his chest. "Are you aware of what you're saying? Not only do you wrong Lord Knarsdale, but you doubt my character."

"No! You misunderstand."

"Hardly. Your words leave no room for misunderstanding."

"Please, Philip, listen to me." Stepping close to her husband, she laid her hands on his stiffly crossed arms and looked up at him. "If I hurt you, I beg your pardon. You are a *good, wonderful* man, and no one knows it better than I. I never intended—Philip, what I meant is that he will manipulate you."

"Indeed, madam." His tone stung. "That, of course, is much more edifying to your husband than saying he'd compromise his values."

She backed away. "What is happening to us? It is bad enough when you scold me, but never before have you lashed out with sarcasm."

"My apologies."

"Philip." Again, she stepped close, but her hands trembled and she did not touch him. "About Lord Knarsdale—"

"I should think you've said quite enough."

"Please hear me out. You're too trusting, Philip. In your goodness, you cannot see the man's true nature."

"Whether or not I lack discernment, Amanda, I assure you I am no man's puppet. Nor would I ever compromise my values."

"Of course not. But Lord Knarsdale—"

"No more!" Philip's voice was stern. He pushed away from the dresser. "It does you no credit to speak disparagingly of the man who has shown us nothing but kindness and generosity."

"He is a schemer. Why can you not see through his facade?"

Philip stood silent and suddenly pale.

Slowly, he turned and walked to the door. She thought he would leave without a word, but he paused. He spoke without looking at her.

"It pains me to have to say this, Amanda. But if you cannot temper your speech . . . and your wholly unjus-

tified dislike of Lord Knarsdale . . . I have no choice but
to leave you here when I return to town in five days."

"What do you mean? *Leave* me here?"

"There is much to be done these next few weeks, and
I cannot be distracted with worries over whom you
might embarrass or insult with your sharp tongue."

"But you cannot leave me *here!* It's preposterous! Utterly unthinkable! I am not a child, to be banished at
will!"

"Then do not act like a child."

"Philip!"

The closing door cut her protest short.

Amanda rushed forward but could not see through
a veil of tears. Her arm brushed against something that
fell with a clatter. She stopped, wiped her eyes with the
sleeve of her nightgown.

Tears again. What on earth was the matter? She never
cried. Or, only for good cause . . . like the loss of her
parents. But the past week or two, she'd had to fight
tears at every contretemps with Philip.

Again, she dashed a sleeve across her eyes. She could
see her way to the door clearly now but made no effort
to follow her husband. It was too late. She had no notion
where he might have gone. This was her first visit to
Darring Court, and when they arrived late last night,
and quite unexpected, the housekeeper had taken them
straight from the great hall through a maze of corridors
and dark stairs to their bedchamber. No candle, or even
the four-branched candelabrum she had knocked off a
small table, would help in a search. For now, Philip was
lost to her.

Lost to her . . .

Tears, wet and cold, rolled unchecked down her face.
Perhaps this was the reason for her crying bouts these
past days . . . she had acknowledged, deep in her heart,

that her bright, happy marriage had turned to ashes.
That she had lost the man she loved.

Amanda spent the rest of the night pacing. When
Philip's watch on the night table showed a half hour
past five o'clock, she placed the last log on the dying
embers in the hearth. Ice-cold water from the pitcher
on the dresser reduced the puffiness around her eyes.
She donned her warmest gown of thick blue wool and
a matching spencer trimmed with black velvet braid.

She hesitated in front of the mirror, but she looked
no better, no worse than any other morning of late.
Pinching her cheeks added color. Her hair, as ordinary
a brown as brown could be, seemed to have more curl
than usual, due, no doubt, to the moist sea air. She practiced a smile, a small trick that more often than not
made her feel better. The dullness of her eyes lightened;
they began to look blue again and lively. She was ready
to face the world. To face Philip?

So much to discuss with him. So many issues to raise.
Even if it meant widening the rift between them . . . tem-
porarily. Surely, their troubles were temporary. Soon,
they would be close again. Their differences and difficulties would come to an end. The horrid thought of
having lost Philip—that sick feeling inside her—was a
result of two days' grueling travel. They loved each
other. She must never forget that.

Armed with a candelabrum, Amanda left the bedchamber without ringing for assistance. Housekeeper
and steward were the only staff in residence until help
was summoned from the village, and that would hardly
happen before daybreak.

The dark, paneled corridor stretched right and left
as far as the candlelight spread, which wasn't far at all.
Amanda had no recollection of their approach to the

chamber last night. She turned left, passing several doors on either side. Presently, the corridor fed into a wider one that crossed her path like the bar of a T. Again, she turned left. No strip of drugget covered the floor here. Her heels tapped loudly on the worn boards. Muted but unmistakable, she heard the howl of the gale again. And the pounding of the sea. Not a sound to endear the house to her.

Amanda walked faster. There were no doors in this corridor, only paintings. Landscapes and portraits, one after the other. Surely, this gallery would lead to a flight of stairs, thence to some lower, inhabited region of this vast, rambling house. To Philip. And to a fire. To a pot of tea.

Instead of the expected stairs, an ornately carved door almost as wide and as high as the passage itself marked the end of the picture gallery. Trying to recall closed doors on the way to her bedchamber the previous night, Amanda pushed down on the brass handle and tugged. The door did not budge, but the key was right there, in the lock.

The key was stiff and would not turn. Amanda set the cumbersome candelabrum down, wriggled the key, and tried again. She thought she felt some slight movement, but whether the key turned or not, the door popped open and thrust against her with a force that sent her reeling backward, against the wall. A gust of cold, moist air doused the candles, rendering the corridor pitch dark. Outside she heard the wind shrieking, howling. The sea crashing, pounding.

Amanda pushed against the door, but now the wretched thing proved as obstinately set against closing as it was formerly against opening. She couldn't just leave it, though. The gale was blowing straight into the gallery, and now that her ears had adjusted to the din outside, she could hear the paintings rattling on the walls.

Then she heard a woman's voice.

"Let me help you."

"Thank you, Mrs. Cobb."

Laughter as airy as silver filigree answered her. A light appeared around the door, and for an instant she was blinded. But the light was lowered immediately. A slight figure wrapped in a long cloak stopped beside her. Small blue-veined hands joined her own firm, capable hands on the door and slowly but steadily closed it against the wind.

"You're not Mrs. Cobb." Breathless from her efforts, Amanda faced the woman who looked no taller nor stronger than a frail twelve-year-old. Even the face was childlike with its delicate features and wide eyes. "Were you outside? But I thought the door was locked!"

"Did you?"

The woman stooped, retrieved her lantern, and it was then that Amanda realized she was addressing a very old lady. Indeed, the face was pink, and delicate as a child's, but beneath the powder lay a gossamer net of fine wrinkles. The woman's eyes, clear and bright, matched the color of her emerald green cloak. Her hair was fine in texture, but it was still full, swept back and up in an elaborate coiffure that shone like a crown of polished copper. It did not look like a wig, but it had to be one. No dye could bring such luster to an old lady's hair.

"I vow it is my own." The woman's eyes sparkled. "And not touched with henna either."

"I beg your pardon. Am I so very transparent?"

"No need to be embarrassed. Everyone wonders who meets me for the first time."

"Who are you? I did not know anyone but the housekeeper was in the house."

"No, how could you? I only just arrived. Shall we re-move to some warmer spot, child?"

"With pleasure. But I don't know where to take you. This is my first visit here, and I'm afraid I don't know my way about yet. I am Amanda Darring."

"Of course you are. Dear Philip's wife."

"You know me? But, surely, I'd remember if we had met before!"

Again the light, silvery laughter. "How true! No one could forget a head like mine."

"I am sorry! I meant no disrespect. I—" Amanda fal-tered. Philip was right. She must think before she spoke.

But the old lady did not look as if she had taken of-fense. She was smiling.

"I am your great-aunt, Sibyl. Or, rather, your hus-band's great-aunt."

"But you're dead!" Amanda blurted out.

"Am I? Strange. I don't feel dead."

"What I mean is that you ought to be dead."

A chuckle made Amanda hasten to add, "There was the letter from Cairo, you see. Philip received it just about a month ago. It was a very proper notification from the consul, who had it firsthand from a Colonel Ledbetter that you were killed in a Bedouin uprising."

"Ledbetter is a fool, and so is our consul. But come along now." Great-aunt Sibyl, lantern in hand, trod sprightly down the corridor. "We'll have Mrs. Cobb make us a nice pot of tea."

"That would be lovely." Retrieving the useless cande-labrum, Amanda followed in all haste.

Suddenly the old lady stopped, raising her lantern to one of the portraits on the wall. "Ha! Still there, I see. And I'd have wagered a fortune that my brother had it removed and burned after my last visit."

"It's you." Amanda stepped close. The hair, the eyes of the girl in the portrait were unmistakable. Even the face, except for the loss of perfect smoothness, had not changed much over the years. "How very, very beautiful you were. And still are."

"Red hair, green eyes, and a wicked propensity for mischief. They called me the Witch of Darring Court."

Two

"But to call you a witch!" said Amanda, not for the first time since Sibyl's pronouncement in the gallery. "How unkind."

"Yet wholly justified," muttered Mrs. Cobb, who had greeted the ladies' appearance in her kitchen with much exclaiming and head shaking, but had nevertheless produced tea and scones and offered the warmth of the kitchen stove.

"Much *you* know about it." Great-aunt Sibyl, near the stove in Mrs. Cobb's own rocking chair, appeared to be enjoying herself hugely. Her eyes danced and sparkled, darting from Amanda to the housekeeper, teasing them, inviting them to enlarge on the topic. "Sixty years ago, when it all started, you were a babe in arms, Mrs. Cobb."

"No need to remind me of my age, madam. My rheumatism does it every morning. And how you, with nigh on a score of years more in your dish, can still find pleasure in junketing about the world, I'll never understand."

"It keeps me young."

Amanda drew her chair closer to Sibyl. "I don't know much about your life, Aunt Sibyl. How did it come about that you traveled so widely?"

"Travel was incidental at first. You see, I married an Italian and, naturally, accompanied my husband when he returned to Rome."

"The *first* husband." Mrs. Cobb plied the pump handle with vigor as she filled a kettle. "And all of a sudden, madam was a countess. A foreign title 'twas, but countess nonetheless. Such an uproar! No worse, though, than the uproar the year before, when she was turning the heads of every young blade in Northumberland."

"Exaggeration," said Sibyl. "But, then, you could not possibly remember those days."

"No, but my sainted mother had stories aplenty to tell. And later, when I was in service in London, I heard more. There wasn't a traveler returning from Italy or France, from Spain or Germany or Russia, who didn't dine out on a tale about you, madam."

"I did move around," Sibyl admitted. "And no matter where I went, my fame, or infamy, depending on the storyteller's point of view, always preceded me."

Mrs. Cobb gave a sniff. " 'Twouldn't have anything to do with the number of husbands you buried, would it? The duels you inspired? The black magic you practiced?"

"Black magic? Never! Not here, nor abroad."

"Nay, and I apologize, madam. Yet, who but a witch could arrive at the break of dawn without me or Mr. Cobb hearing the cart or seeing a bit of luggage?"

"No sorcery in that, my dear Mrs. Cobb. It was all the work of my devoted Abdul."

"Abdul?" Enthralled, Amanda leaned toward the older woman. "That's an Arabian name. Then you *are* married to a Bedouin prince? There was some speculation, you see. *Before* the report of your death."

Sibyl laughed. "Perhaps I am married; perhaps I'm not. Again, it depends on the point of view. But, although I shall leave it to him to affirm or deny that he is a prince, I can assure you with absolute certainty that Abdul is not my husband."

"Madam!" Mrs. Cobb had stopped in the act of feeding coal into the stove and turned, bristling with indignation. "Do I understand that you brought a heathen into the house? At this time of the year? Have you forgot it's All Hallows Even tomorrow?"

"So it is, Mrs. Cobb." In the firelight, Sibyl's hair looked flaming red. "And from your demeanor, I take it that the old nonsense is still going on?"

"Aye. And it curdles the blood of a good Christian, it does. And you bringing a heathen! *I* shan't be here tomorrow night, but the master and his wife will be. Have you no regard for them, madam?"

"My dear Mrs. Cobb! Abdul may be a heathen, but he is not a pagan."

"Pagan! Heathen!" The housekeeper slammed the stove door. "What's the difference, I ask? But never mind a clever explanation."

Sibyl smiled. "No, indeed. You wouldn't listen anyway."

"What does Abdul have to do with Halloween?" asked Amanda.

"Nothing at all, my dear." Sibyl reached for the teapot on the stove and refilled the cups. "Mrs. Cobb is confusing Muhammadanism with paganism."

Snatching her shawl from a chair, the housekeeper marched to the yard entrance. "I'm off to the village to fetch help. If you need anything you'll have to go for Cobb. You'll find him in the woodshed."

The yard door closed not much more gently than the stove door.

Amanda smiled at Sibyl. "You created quite a stir, ma'am."

"I always do. But so, I believe, do you. At least every now and again?"

"Gracious! You've heard about me?" Amanda felt queasy all of a sudden, the scone she had eaten, a lump in her stomach. "I did not think I was that bad! I do not guard my tongue, I know. Philip says I lack discretion. That I must think before I speak. But, great heavens! I did not realize that reports of my wretched tongue had gone abroad!"

"They haven't. It just so happened—but never mind. Tell me, where is Philip? Perhaps we should share these delicious scones and offer him a cup of tea."

"Yes. Yes, of course." Amanda rose. She felt hot, then cold, then rather ill. "I don't know where he is. He left me in the night, and I have no notion where to look for him."

"He'll be in the study, I dare say. That was where I could always find him on those occasions he and I both happened to visit here."

Amanda stood on trembling legs. She was shaking all over. How silly to be so apprehensive about her next meeting with Philip. Best get it over with.

"The study . . . Aunt Sibyl, where is it?"

When Sibyl rose, Amanda took an unsteady step toward her. "No need to trouble yourself, ma'am. Just give me directions, please."

With surprising strength, the older woman propelled Amanda back into the chair.

"Stay right here, child. If anyone goes in search of Philip, it shall be me. You look as if you're about to swoon."

"I never swoon. And I'm better already."

But Amanda did not try to rise again. She wanted Philip. She wanted to put matters to rights between them. Knowing, however, that his greeting this morning, in the smoothest, most reasonable tone, would be, "Well, my dear? Have you given due consideration to my words?" was enough to make her feel quite ill again. What *was* there to consider in his ultimatum? She would not, *absolutely not,* stay behind on an island. But neither could she promise that she would not ever speak against Lord Knarsdale again.

"Drink this," said Sibyl. "Plain tea. No cream or sugar this time."

It seemed simplest to obey that compassionate but firm voice, and, amazingly, the tea did make Amanda feel better.

"How far along are you?" asked Sibyl.

"How far . . . ?" Amanda frowned. "I'm sorry. I feel quite extraordinarily stupid. What did you ask me?"

"How far along you are. When a young, healthy woman who shows no signs of a fever or other ailment, feels faint and ill, the inevitable conclusion must be drawn that she is expecting."

"Impossible!"

"Is it, my dear?"

Amanda was silent, distracted.

After a moment, Sibyl said, "Impertinent of me to question you, I realize. But I never gave a fig for the conventions, and I'm not about to change. So, if you wish to share whatever is troubling you, I am at your disposal. If not, just tell me to mind my own business."

"I will."

"I don't doubt it in the least." Sibyl's voice held laughter. "And Philip? How does he react to your refreshing candor?"

Amanda's eyes widened.

"No need to answer, child. Again, I can draw my own conclusion."

"How can you draw a conclusion, ma'am? You don't know me at all, and Philip, by your own admission, only from a few meetings."

"But those meetings—also his letters—allow me a fair assessment of his personality. And if there is one subject I understand very well, it is the male species. When a man of some thirty-odd years marries a girl who hasn't reached her eighteenth year—"

"Philip was twenty-eight when we married."

"I stand corrected. But Philip was always older than his years, and I am trying to point out that the very same qualities which enchant and captivate a man when he finds them in a very young girl, are the qualities he will wish to change the most when he sees them in his wife of some years."

"Almost ten years." Amanda saw kindness and wisdom in Sibyl's eyes. "And for more than eight of those years, Philip found no fault in me. But, perhaps I *should* change. He is no longer a country parson, and we no longer live where everyone has known me since the day I was born."

"Yes, Philip wrote that you moved to town. Amanda, do you not enjoy London?"

"Oh, very much! And the work we do—did he write about Magdalen Home? And about our schools?"

"Indeed, he did. You provide suitable training and find respectable posts for unfortunate females who wish to reform. And at your schools, you board and educate every waif you can snatch off the streets. My brother— Philip's grandfather—would turn over in his grave if he knew to what purpose Philip is putting his inheritance."

"I hope he does know. 'Twould serve him right for the odd stipulations in his will."

Sibyl gazed into her teacup, tilting it this way and that, as if fascinated by the dregs in the bottom of the cup. "Why is it impossible that you are expecting?"

Amanda rose and slowly traversed the length of the kitchen. At the stone sink with the low, deep-set window behind it, she stopped. Daylight had broken, but there was not a hint of sun, only pale grayness with diaphanous tufts of fog floating close to the cobbled ground. Amanda's back was toward Sibyl. Very slowly, very gently,

Amanda placed both hands on her abdomen and stood thus for a few moments.

Her hands dropped. It was impossible.

She turned. "They told me I am barren."

"Who? Some quack physician?"

"I saw three London doctors of great repute. One was Sir Richard Croft, Princess Charlotte's own physician."

"And much good he did for her! She died, didn't she? And her babe, too."

Again, Amanda spread a hand against her abdomen. Her eyes were on Sibyl, but she did not see the older woman in the rocking chair. She saw a crib, a babe, all curled up and sleeping . . .

What if it were possible?

"What about your monthly flow?" asked Sibyl.

Amanda blinked, saw the older woman rocking gently. Sibyl's wide green eyes were clear and sharp, and seemed to look straight into her mind. What a fanciful thought! Worthy of a pregnant woman.

Amanda gave herself a mental shake. Her monthly flow . . . how long had it been? "Three months or so. But it means nothing. I've always been irregular—immature female organs, the physicians said. It is the reason I will never conceive."

"And how long have you been unwell?"

"A mere few days. And only when I think of Philip." Amanda's face flamed. "I beg your pardon! I did not mean that as it must have sounded."

"Of course not, child. I've already disregarded it."

"Thank you." To her consternation, Amanda burst into tears.

Sibyl left the rocking chair. She handed Amanda a handkerchief. "And how long have you suffered weeping spells?"

"About two weeks." Amanda blew her nose. "Maybe three."

"Yet you still say it's impossible that you're expecting?"

Amanda thought back over the past weeks, back to a night in early September when Philip last shared her bed. That would have been about seven weeks ago. Her breath caught.

"I suppose," she whispered, "it is possible after all."

Sibyl nodded. "You have all the signs."

Amanda's eyes, so doubtful at first, glowed as excitement ignited and spread like fire on a dry heath. "Good gracious, Aunt Sibyl! It is quite, totally, entirely possible! It is *more* than possible!"

Sibyl laughed. "Even had you denied it, I'd still have sent a christening gift in less than nine months' time. Child, there isn't much that escapes my eye."

"No, indeed. And if I hadn't given up all hope . . . if I hadn't been distracted by another matter, I would have recognized that I don't at all feel the way I usually feel when the flow is merely delayed."

Amanda hugged Sibyl, then twirled around the kitchen. She felt light as air, bubbling with joy. She knew, as certainly as if she had gone through pregnancy before, that she was, indeed, with child. How blessed she was! A child after ten years of marriage!

Sibyl went to the dresser at the back of the kitchen, where she had set down her lantern. "I suppose, now you will want me to show you to the study with all haste."

"Oh, yes! This instant!" Amanda twirled toward the arched doorway through which they had entered, hours ago, or so it seemed. "Philip will be ecstatic! He will—"

Amanda came to an abrupt halt. "No."

"*No?* What is the matter, my dear? Does Philip not want a child?"

"I cannot tell Philip just now." Jerkily, Amanda turned her back on the archway. "I want to wait—something to settle first."

Sibyl raised a brow, but before she could demand enlightenment, footsteps came down the stone staircase that led from the main floor to the butler's pantry adjoining the kitchen. Footsteps, Amanda knew very well. Heart pounding, she faced the archway and waited.

Handsome and distinguished-looking even in boots, breeches, and an old, worn riding coat, Philip entered the kitchen. Her husband. Her love.

The father of her child. Their child.

"Good morning, Amanda. I suspected I might find you here."

"Good morning, Philip." How calm he was. How stern. And how utterly self-assured, while she was once more tongue-tied. But this time, it was the stirring of her conscience that robbed her of words. How could she even think of not telling him the good news immediately!

"Well, my dear? Have you weighed and considered the matter we discussed in the night?"

She scanned his face for some small sign of anxiety or inner turmoil, but his expression was calm, his look inscrutable. "There is nothing to weigh or consider. Your demands are most unreasonable."

"I am sorry to hear it. You leave me no choice—"

"Philip!" cried Sibyl, tripping toward them. "How are you, dear boy? Oh, how I have missed you!"

Only a slight quirk of his dark brows betrayed astonishment. Then he smiled. "Indeed, Aunt Sibyl? Is that the reason you stayed away a dozen years or more? But I am delighted to see you alive and well. Are you aware that the consul in Cairo alarmed us with a report of your death?"

"He is a fool. And how gullible you are! You may believe that I am dead when you receive my ring along with a report." Sibyl held out a hand, adorned with a

star sapphire of magnificent size and surrounded by
seven large diamonds.

Amanda stared, wondering how she could have over-
looked such a ring when Sibyl helped her close the door
in the picture gallery.

Sibyl smiled at her. "It shall be yours, child. The stone
is the exact color of your eyes."

Proffering a delicately powdered cheek to Philip,
Sibyl demanded his kiss, then stood back to gaze fondly
up at him. "How marvelous that your visit here coin-
cides with mine!"

"Marvelous, indeed." Any trace of sternness had disappeared from Philip's face. His smile was warm, almost
boyish. "Only, I don't like to believe in coincidence. Do
you, Aunt Sibyl?"

"Of course not. It was merely a figure of speech. You
know very well I always direct my broomstick when and
where to go."

"Your broomstick?" he said quizzingly. "You disappoint me sadly. I was sure that after all your travels in
the East you must have found a flying carpet at least, or
some other magical device more romantic than a broomstick."

Amanda stared at her husband. This was the man she
had fallen in love with, the man who allowed a teasing
note in his voice, who let a hint of laughter show in his
eyes, who was not above responding to a bit of nonsense.
This was the man she had scarcely seen since they moved
to London.

With obvious delight, Sibyl said, "You read the *Arabian Nights' Entertainments*. How wonderful! It proves
you're not so starchy that you're past redemption. But
wherever did you find a copy of those splendid tales,
Philip?"

"On your night table, dear Aunt. Twenty years ago.
You offered me the use of your traveling library."

Sibyl chuckled. "I remember now. You had spent most of your vacation poring over thick theological tomes. I thought it was time you had a bit of fun before you resumed your studies."

"I did have fun. Always . . . when your visits coincided with my vacation."

"But you don't believe in coincidence, Philip."

"No, indeed," he said warmly. "And I am well aware that you planned it all. You did not visit Darring Court as often as I, but every one of your stays was scheduled during my long vacation. Aunt Sibyl—" Philip's face changed, became inscrutable again. "You said something earlier. Something about me, being starchy but not beyond redemption?"

"Did I?" Sibyl turned to Amanda. "Have we eaten all the scones, my dear, or might there be one left for Philip?"

"More than one. I saw Mrs. Cobb hide a batch. Soul cakes, too, which Philip likes." Glad of an excuse to move about, Amanda went and peeked into the warming oven. "No doubt, these are for Mr. Cobb. How many shall I filch for you, Philip?"

"It is hardly *filching*," he said with dampening sobriety, "when you serve me from the Darring Court larders."

Amanda closed the oven door. "Philip, we must talk."

"Can it wait until—" He paused and frowned at her. "Amanda, are you quite well? You look a little peaked. Perhaps you should lie down."

"No. I want to talk to you."

"My dear, if it is about our discussion last night, there is nothing more to add."

Her hands clenched. "We did not discuss *anything*. You gave me an ultimatum and walked out."

"Amanda—" His voice was pained. "Must we air our

differences in front of Aunt Sibyl? She'll think us a sad pair of ragamuffins."

"Pish! Aunt Sibyl was married several times. She will not be shocked to witness an argument."

"You're correct. Because there will be no argument." Sibyl said, "Don't hold back on my account. You should have seen the sparks fly when my first husband and I had a difference of opinion!"

"Be that as it may." Philip's voice was bland. "There will be no sparks here."

A dangerous glint lit in Amanda's eyes. "And how, pray tell, will you avoid it? Unless—Philip, are you prepared to withdraw your demands?"

"Not at all. I shall simply remove myself from the scene." He bowed. "Ladies, I wish you a pleasant morning."

"No!" cried Amanda. "You cannot walk out again!"

But he could. Quite calmly, Philip strode to the yard door.

"Do you know, Philip," Sibyl said cheerfully to his back, "you bring to mind my third husband. Such a handsome man. Such a stiff and sober Prussian. So proper and so . . . depressing."

Philip gave her a strange look, pensive and a little puzzled. He bowed again and left.

Unlike the housekeeper earlier, Philip shut the door very gently. Nevertheless, the all but inaudible click of the latch held a note of finality that immediately had Amanda in tears.

"Detestable!" She dabbed her eyes. "And I don't even know which I mean—Philip's craven departure or these infernal tears."

"A little of both, I imagine." Sibyl took Amanda's arm. "Come, let me show you the quickest way to your chamber. And when you have rested, I shall give you the grand tour. The view of the sea from the outside gallery will take your breath away."

Amanda suppressed a shudder but said politely, "I daresay it'll be spectacular. On a stormy day like this."

"What strange notions you have, my dear. This is not a storm. 'Tis the merest bluster."

Three

Amanda was too restless to stay in her chamber and begged Sibyl to show her over the house at once, then regretted it almost immediately. The rooms were cold and dusty, most of the furnishings shrouded in Holland covers. The confusion of dark passages that turned sharply or ended unexpectedly served only to heighten Amanda's agitation. She could not like the hundred-fifty-year-old seat of the Darring family. And since she knew that Philip had no affinity for the place where, perforce, he had spent every school vacation after his parents' death in a tragic carriage mishap, she wished they had never come on this visit.

Even the longed-for closeness to Philip, within grasp during the first few hours in their chamber, seemed more impossible than ever. His trunk, she had discovered, was now in a room two doors from hers.

"You are frowning," said Sibyl. "That is not good. If you want a happy, contented child, you must have happy thoughts."

Amanda forced a smile. How could she be happy as long as she kept the joyous news from Philip? Yet how could she share it when he was planning to leave her in this ancient house—for how long? There was a vacancy in the House of Commons. Lord Knarsdale believed he could get Philip elected. And then? Would

Philip Darring, M.P., wish to see his outspoken wife back in London?

Sibyl said, "Let us fetch our cloaks and go outside. The wind will sweep the cobwebs from your mind."

"As long as we're not swept away as well!"

Sibyl's cloak was still in the kitchen, and from there she led the way up the narrow steps of an enclosed back stairwell to the second floor and to Amanda's chamber. Moments later, warmly wrapped, the ladies opened the heavy carved door that had proven so troublesome earlier in the morning.

Immediately, they were caught by the gale, whipping at their cloaks and making them flap like sails on a floundering ship. The gray, turbulent North Sea spread as far as the eye could see, high white-capped waves swelling, rolling, crashing . . . swelling, rolling, crashing . . . without cease. The sight was enough to make Amanda dizzy. And the din! That horrid sound of waves breaking on the cliffs directly below the gallery grated on her nerves.

"Isn't it glorious?" Sibyl allowed her hood to slip. She drifted to the stone balustrade, face toward the sky, arms spread wide, as if she wished to embrace the elements. "I feel as if I could take off like a bird, and fly."

"I feel tossed about, like a hapless piece of flotsam." Amanda retreated until her back pressed against the house wall. "Pray step back, Aunt Sibyl. That balustrade is far too low for safety."

Sibyl turned. "Don't be afraid, child. We're quite safe, I promise you. Many a night have I slept out here as a young girl. Calm or storm, it made no difference. Come, take my hand. I'll hold you steady."

Amanda was not a tall woman, but Sibyl was smaller, and the notion of a frail old lady as the anchor to safety did nothing to reassure Amanda—until she met Sibyl's clear gaze. There was something about the older woman that inspired confidence and trust. Perhaps it was an inner strength Sibyl had, a conviction that she was mistress of her life.

Amanda pushed away from the wall. "I apologize for my cowardice. For some inexplicable reason I do not like the sea, which is why I did not accompany Philip before."

"And you need never come again. The terms of my brother's will demand the obligatory visit only from Philip."

"Such a strange stipulation. If he chooses not to live here, he must visit at least once every year, on Halloween. Philip did not explain why. Do you know the reason?"

"I'll show you. We are now on the east side or the back of the house, and we'll follow the gallery to the north side."

The two ladies walked side by side, Sibyl close to the balustrade, where she could enjoy the full force of the wind. Since Darring Court was built on the outermost tip of Raven Island, the south and east walls of the house rose directly above the cliffs. Along the north side of the house stretched a small park, and the west or main front of Darring Court faced a hamlet of some forty-odd cottages, beyond which, on a clear day at low tide, could be seen a track connecting the island to the mainland. This track had been covered by a churning sea when Amanda and Philip arrived and had necessitated a nerve-racking boat ride.

"When is low tide?" asked Amanda.

"At present, between four o'clock and six, mornings and evenings. It's when the cart can cross with deliveries. Or visitors."

"The cart Mrs. Cobb did not hear when you arrived?"

Sibyl laughed. "I am a witch, am I not?"

"How I envy you. I had to ride in a boat."

For a while they walked in silence, sometimes struggling against the wind, sometimes being propelled by it. Once, Sibyl pointed out the two small mullioned windows of Amanda's chamber.

"Gracious!" said Amanda when they had turned several corners, some sharp, some rounded. "The house is bad enough inside, but out here! So many nooks and crannies. I cannot help but think the architect had lost his wits."

"Not at all. When the house was built, Scottish marauders still attacked with regularity, and thus two sides of the house were designed to conform precisely to the outline of the cliffs below. This meant security. Look." Hair in wild disarray, Sibyl leaned over the balustrade. "There's no path, no track, where men could gather and attack."

"I shall take your word for it."

"You look chilled." Once more, Sibyl strode into the wind. "Not much farther, child. Just around the next corner."

Amanda followed more slowly, admiring the older woman's stamina, her capacity for enjoyment. In London, she had been like Sibyl, energetic, vibrant. Despite the growing rift between her and Philip, she had found great pleasure in their work. The schools they had founded, the women's home, were a constant challenge. Like Sibyl striding into the wind and enjoying the struggle, so had Amanda forged ahead, reveling in every small victory won, in every setback overcome.

Here, on Raven Island, she was indeed like flotsam. Tossed about, incapable of steering a course.

Pregnant. And she had not yet told Philip.

Despite herself, Amanda glanced to the right, at the sea. The waves were still a dizzying sight. She did, with grudging respect, acknowledge the majestic power that had once carried the Vikings to Britain's shore. But not for a moment could she forget that the cold, churning waters totally surrounded her.

No, she could not—would not—stay behind when Philip left for London.

Rounding the next corner, Amanda saw a strip of rock-strewn beach and part of the Darring Court park. Perhaps park was a misnomer. It was not much larger than a country garden, and there were few trees and shrubs, stunted and gnarled, trunks and bare branches bent toward the mainland.

"There used to be flower beds," said Sibyl, looking unusually wistful. "The chrysanthemums were beautiful around Halloween. Roses and lilies in the summer. Tulips in the spring. So many tulips. Enough to put Holland to shame."

"Would you live here again?" asked Amanda. "Put everything in order?"

"No, child. But, look! Can you see the churchyard beyond the park? And that wide rock jutting into the sea like a giant thumb?"

"Someone is building a bonfire on the rock!" Forgetting her reservations, Amanda leaned against the balustrade. "It is huge! There's a man climbing a ladder to add to the top."

"When the bonfire is lit, the sight is most spectacular from the sea."

"I'd be glad to view it from up here." Amanda caught her hood as the wind tugged at it. "But we'll be gone by Mischief Night."

"So you will. If Philip isn't vigilant, however, you'll see the fire burn on All Hallows Even."

"I beg pardon? What does Philip—" Amanda saw a rider slowly round the enormous stack of wood. There was no mistaking the proud dark head, the straight back. It was Philip.

He used to take pleasure in her company when he

rode out . . . and she, in his. Of course, there was the baby to consider now, and riding, some said, could cause a miscarriage. It was such a miracle that she had conceived at all, she would do nothing to jeopardize the pregnancy.

But Philip had not even suggested that she accompany him.

Two men walked beside the horse. They seemed to be arguing with Philip. He shook his head and rode off.

Sibyl said, "Those two are probably men from the mainland. They bring oak limbs, which we don't have here."

"Aunt Sibyl . . . what did you mean by 'if Philip isn't vigilant'?"

"He is the guardian of the bonfire. He must make sure it isn't lit on Halloween but stays intact till Mischief Night."

Amanda was watching Philip as he entered the park and rode toward the stable yard, but now she turned incredulous eyes on Sibyl.

"Is *that* the reason we're here? To guard a stack of wood? How ridiculous! What was his grandfather thinking of when he made his will?"

"A Darring has stood watch on Halloween night for nigh on seventy years to stop those who'd want to light the bonfire then."

"Why, for goodness' sake? Even though most of us eschew Halloween for Guy Fawkes Day, it is not a crime or treason to follow the more ancient customs."

"No," Sibyl said quietly, "it is not a crime as long as the customs remain harmless fun. But you must forgive my brother's crotchets. You see, a few of the island families and many more on the mainland are connected to a Scottish village just across the border, where Samhain, the Celtic Lord of the Dead, is worshiped on All Hallows Even."

"Ah! Now, Mrs. Cobb's reference to paganism is beginning to make sense. And when you spoke of oak branches for the bonfire—the oak was sacred to the Celts, was it not? But are you saying that families *here*—"

"Celebrate Celtic rites?" Sibyl was silent for a moment. "There were rumors. Charred animal bones were found in the ashes."

"How horrid! *The Times* reported such finds at Stonehenge last Halloween. But *here!* I shall certainly help Philip stand guard. There is nothing more barbaric than animal sacrifice!"

Sibyl looked at her, and something in the older woman's expression, a sudden stillness and withdrawal, made Amanda catch her breath.

"Oh, no! Aunt Sibyl, surely not! Pray tell me that I am letting my imagination run amok."

"Indeed, you are, child." Sibyl smiled and was her bright, cheerful self again. "But I blame myself. I have never been able to tell a straight fact, always adding a note of drama, which you caught."

Amanda breathed easier. And yet, she could have sworn that, for a moment, Sibyl had been overcome by dark memories.

She said, a little doubtfully, "You were teasing me then? There are no pagan rites? No charred animal bones?"

"What I should have said is that my brother started the watch. Even as a very young man, he had a Puritan streak and an overabundance of religious fervor. He abhorred anything that smacked of paganism. He was a strict adherent to the Church of England, and since Halloween as a Christian festival was sanctioned by the Catholic Church—well, you can imagine his distaste. He was determined to save the bonfire for Mischief Night. To torch Guy Fawkes' effigy."

Amanda studied her companion. "I think you're

keeping something back. Did your brother start guarding the bonfire because people called you a witch?"

"Oh, no. I was only a child when he set up the watch." Sibyl suddenly looked mischievous. "But he was horrified when the witch rumors started. And he never forgave me."

"He blamed you? How odd he must have been. Well, he *was* odd. He never wanted to meet me."

"The stubborn old fool."

"But I still believe you're not telling me everything. I shan't press you, though. No doubt you feel you must spare me on account of my delicate condition."

"And your delicate condition demands a rest and nourishment. If Mrs. Cobb does not return soon—but there she is!" Sibyl pointed to the cart track from the village. "With three helpers. Just in time to prepare a luncheon."

Amanda, however, had once more caught sight of her husband, who had stabled his horse and was striding toward the house. Forgotten was the bonfire, the strange tale Sibyl had told.

"Excuse me, Aunt Sibyl. I must speak with Philip."

Amanda did not heed Sibyl calling after her but ran back the way they had come, entered through the gallery door, and burst unceremoniously into the chamber where she had earlier seen Philip's trunk.

Philip wasn't there, and so she waited, pacing the floor. She unfastened her cloak but kept it on, for no fire was laid; there was not even a wood basket or a bucket of coal. Surely Mr. Cobb's morning in the woodshed should have produced some fuel for the master's chamber.

She waited for what seemed like a very long time. Long enough to mull over the threat Philip had made in the night. That he would leave her here if she could not temper her speech and her dislike of Lord Knarsdale.

Temper her speech . . . she could do that, if she must. But there would still be a slight problem. Philip's notion of temperance would not be the same as hers.

Temper her dislike of a man she despised . . . that was impossible. And, therefore, she would be left behind in a house she hadn't wanted to visit in the first place; on an island, where she would be imprisoned by the cold North Sea.

Unless she told Philip about the baby.

He would never leave her behind if he knew she was expecting. He wouldn't even insist any longer that she must change her ways. He would wish that she did, but he would not demand it.

She would demand it of herself. And that would be a steep price to pay for choosing the coward's way.

But silence also cost her dearly. She could not fully savor the joy of her pregnancy unless she shared the news with Philip.

She heard his footsteps in the corridor, and before she could decide what to say and whether to sit or remain standing, he entered the chamber.

"Philip, I've been waiting for you."

"So I see."

She crossed to the door and leaned against it. "You shall not walk out on me again until we have spoken."

"My dear, I have no intention of leaving." Sitting on the edge of the four-poster bed, he started to pull off his boots. "I must wash and change. And then—would you lend a hand here? These boots are a trifle snug."

She complied, tugging first one, then the other riding boot off his feet. "Why did you not bring Roberts? Or Mary, for that matter?"

"I am sorry if you're inconvenienced without your maid."

"I am not. Do you know, I miss it sometimes . . . the privacy we used to have before we could afford maids and menservants."

He stretched his toes. "I daresay Mrs. Cobb can find a girl for you."

"That is not necessary."

"But easily arranged."

"Truly, Philip! In the three years since you sold your grandfather's coal mines I have not become so useless or spoiled that I cannot do without a maid."

Philip strode to the wash table. He tested the water in the pitcher and, with a grimace, poured some into the bowl. "A maid or manservant would have come mighty handy. But I cannot blame Mrs. Cobb for the lack of service since I arrived two days before I was expected."

"Because of what I said to Lord Knarsdale?"

He did not reply, and she said, "You can ring for hot water. Mrs. Cobb has returned with help from the village."

"This will do." Philip shrugged out of his coat, tossed it and his cravat onto the bed. He rolled up his shirt-sleeves, then hastily performed the ablutions.

Deeming it foolish to insist on a continuance of their conversation while Philip was gritting his teeth, Amanda strolled about the room. It was a sad sight, the wood paneling marred with dry rot, the bossed friezes gray with dust.

When she saw him reach for a towel, she said, "Philip, I would like very much to know why you married me."

Four

Philip turned, the towel halfway to his dripping face. *"What* did you say?"

"Why did you marry me?"

He dried off quickly, perfunctorily. Tossing the towel aside, he crossed the room.

"Because I fell in love with you." Taking her hands, he drew them against his chest. "Amanda, I loved you when I married you. And, God help me, I love you now. You must believe that."

"If you loved me . . . as you should love your wife . . . the woman who would be not only lover but companion, helpmeet, friend, then you would not be so obsessed with changing me."

"It is because I do want you to be everything to me that some maturity on your part is necessary." He held her hands more firmly. "I have wondered of late whether the difference in our ages is, perhaps, too much."

"For goodness' sake, Philip! You make it sound as if you were a graybeard and snatched me from the cradle."

"You had only just turned seventeen when we married."

"But I did not stay that young. Whether you acknowledge it or not, I have aged ten years. *I have matured, Philip!"*

"Have you? Then why not practice reticence, a little more discretion in your speech?"

"True, I still say what comes to mind. But I am not a feather-brained young girl. And if you listened, truly listened when I speak, you'd know it is not empty chatter."

He was silent, a frown gathering in his dark eyes.

"Philip, do consider! I am old enough—have been married long enough to be the mother of a nine-year-old. If we'd had a child in the first year of our marriage, would you not be looking at me differently now?"

"If we'd had a child—" His breath caught. "Then you still think about it."

"Philip . . . don't *you*?"

She read the answer in his eyes and all but blurted out the news to him, but he was speaking already.

He said, with a crooked smile, "I have sixty-three children to love and to teach. And so do you. Surely, that is enough for any couple?"

"And yet you would deprive me of them and leave me here."

He released her hands abruptly.

"Philip, why must I change what drew you to me? I have not caused you harm with my frank speech—except, perhaps, in your own mind. And Lord Knarsdale's."

"It is best, I think, if we leave Knarsdale out of this discussion."

"Oh, very well. In any case, I was speaking of when we fell in love. You know you wouldn't have looked twice at me had I been an insipid, quiet maiden."

"I shouldn't have looked at you at all. I was the vicar. I confirmed you."

She could not help it; she burst out laughing. "That is precisely what Mama said!"

"Amanda, this is no laughing matter. Your parents had already chosen a very suitable young man for you."

"As your grandfather had chosen your bride. Do you regret marrying against his wishes?"

"Of course not."

Philip went to his trunk at the foot of the bed and pulled out pantaloons, a waistcoat, and a bottle-green coat. He seemed to consider their conversation at an end; not so, Amanda.

"Philip, it was Lord Knarsdale's sister your grandfather chose, was it not?"

He turned. "Who told you? I am sure I never mentioned it."

"You did not." Amanda hesitated. "Were you betrothed?"

"No. And I don't think we need discuss Lord Knarsdale's sister."

"I am not discussing her. I do not even know the lady. But she is connected to Lord Knarsdale—yes, yes, I know!" She held up a hand, acknowledging the tightening of his mouth. "I may not mention him either!"

"Then, if you're quite done with the subject, I had best change for luncheon. And you, my dear, may wish to dress your hair."

Even as her hands flew to the offending curls, which, indeed, were disheveled from the wind and the heavy hood of her cloak, Amanda said indignantly, "No, I am not done. And I will speak the forbidden name again. I must, for it is he who caused the rift between us."

"Amanda!" he warned.

"It was Knarsdale, who labeled my tongue 'sharp.' "

"With reason."

"How unjust, Philip! Have you had complaints from anyone else? It is Knarsdale, who has been telling you that I will be a detriment to your political career. That I will insult your colleagues, will gossip, spread rumors."

"He has your welfare in mind. He fears you will be ostracized."

"And you believe him! Philip, do you know how much that hurts?"

"I regret that I caused you pain." He took a step toward her, stopped, saying stiffly, "Perhaps you think none of this affects me."

"And does it, Philip?" she asked quietly. "Are you as miserable as I am? Then, perhaps, Lord Knarsdale is right. He said his sister would have made you a better wife."

"Madam, you have said enough!"

"Not yet. Philip, if I am such a handicap, I wish you *had* married her and spared yourself the misery. But there's no help for it now. You are a man of the cloth and cannot divorce me to take a more suitable wife."

Philip, whose calm was legendary, flung his change of clothing onto the bed. He gripped her shoulders, his eyes blazing with anger.

"Don't *ever* say that again. I love you, Amanda! And *nothing* will ever change that."

"Then why—" She broke off, shaken and confused.

She had spoken the truth, but, perhaps, sometimes, the truth had best remain unspoken. Never had she seen Philip so angry, but whether it was with her or with himself was impossible to tell. He had all but shouted that he loved her. And she believed him. But love, it appeared, was not what could save a love match from turning into the sham an arranged marriage was from the very beginning.

She started to speak but thought better of it. Philip was still struggling to control his emotions, and for once she'd hold her tongue.

His grip on her shoulders eased, as did the harshness of his breathing.

"Forgive me." He stepped away from her. "I did not mean to treat you harshly."

A mere few inches separated them. To Amanda they seemed an unbridgeable gulf.

"I am not made of glass, Philip. And I did provoke you."

He shook his head but said no more. Though neither of them moved, the distance between them seemed to widen.

But she knew what she must do.

"Philip—" Her voice shook, and those infernal tears were coursing down her cheeks again. "There is something you must know."

"Don't weep," he said tiredly. "I shan't leave you here, if that is what you fear."

"You won't?" Her eyes widened. "Truly, Philip? You won't?"

"I have thought about it and decided—"

"You won't!" With a hiccough, half sob, half laughter, she flung her arms around him. "Why didn't you say so right away? The things I said to you! The horrid, bleak thoughts I had!"

"My dear, you are precipitate."

The quietness of his voice chilled her. A sick flutter started in her stomach, and her arms slipped from his neck.

"I am? But you just said it. And you assured me that you still love me!"

"When we leave here, I shall take you to your uncle. Only until I have found a house. If I settle you near your relations, your old friends, you will not dislike living in the country."

She could not speak, did not even try, but turned and left his chamber.

If Amanda and Philip had been alone at Darring Court, she might have stayed in her own room until it was time to depart. Or she might not. Her emotions were in such turmoil, she could not tell from one moment to the next what she felt. She was devastated. She was angry. Furious. Heartbroken. She was ready to fight Philip every mile of the way to her uncle's house. She wanted to cry. Never see him again. Wanted to shake him and tell him about the baby.

But she had no choice whether or not to see Philip. There was Aunt Sibyl, and no matter what Amanda's preferences were, she would not be impolite or disrespectful to her husband's aunt.

The afternoon passed quietly, as did the evening, in a semblance of ordinariness. Undoubtedly, it helped that Sibyl was in an expansive mood and whiled away the hours after dinner with tales of adventure and the more ridiculous mishaps during her recent travels in the East.

When Philip lighted the ladies' way upstairs shortly after ten o'clock, he said, "And this Abdul you spoke of, why has he not shown his face all day, Aunt Sibyl? Perhaps, if he served our meals, I would not have soup on my coat or you salmon on your gown."

"No, indeed. But Abdul is a very private man. I doubt you'll catch a glimpse of him at all. Good night, Philip." Sibyl stopped at the large corner apartment, consisting of a bedroom, a sitting room, and a dressing room. It was the apartment given her for life, according to the terms of her brother's will. "Sleep well, Amanda, my dear."

"You, too, Aunt Sibyl."

Amanda hurried to her own chamber before Sibyl's door had closed. A few moments later, she heard Philip's footsteps. They slowed just outside her room, stopped, then moved on. She heard his door close. Heart pounding, she listened awhile, but all was quiet. He did not return. And, perhaps, it was for the best. She had nothing to say to him.

Except that he would be a father. But that must wait. Or should it?

The night brought no counsel, and when she awoke feeling rather queasy the next morning, Amanda gladly postponed going downstairs. She'd just as soon miss breakfast altogether as face the sight of eggs or the deviled kidneys Philip would undoubtedly be eating.

Yet, if he knew, he'd be considerate. He would spare her the sight of anything she could not fancy.

At nine o'clock, she opened her door. It was Halloween. Surely, by now Philip would have gone riding or guarding the bonfire, or whatever it was his grandfather's ridiculous will ordered him to do.

Pausing at Sibyl's rooms, Amanda knocked, even peeked inside. There was no one. She turned away and all but jumped at the sight of a dark man in a loose white robe, a white cloth flowing from the top of his head to his shoulders. He stood in the corridor a mere few feet from her, yet she had not heard his approach.

She gathered her wits. "You must be Abdul."

He did not speak or move but stood right in her path, a tall, powerful looking man of indeterminable age.

Remembering Sibyl's tales, Amanda placed her right palm on her forehead and bowed. *"Salaam."*

"Good morning, madam. You will find Lady Sibyl downstairs partaking of breakfast. Will you kindly tell her that you saw me?"

"You do speak English!"

"I attended Queen's College. Oxford, madam."

"Oh. Well, it is a pleasure meeting you, Abdul."

He bowed, moved past her soundlessly. When she turned, he was already gone, the door to Sibyl's chambers closed.

Bemused, Amanda went downstairs. What a strange

servant Sibyl had. Perhaps she could be persuaded to tell his story. But when Amanda reached the dining room, both Philip and Sibyl were there, and she forgot Abdul in the effort it took to control her emotions when she heard Philip's deep, warm laughter at something Sibyl had said. How dare he laugh when she was miserable! When he had deprived her of that rich, wonderful sound all these past months in London.

But she smiled at both, kissed Sibyl's proffered cheek, and allowed Philip to seat her at the table. And he thought she could not temper her speech!

"Tea?" Sibyl handed her a cup. No sugar. No cream.

"Thank you. But, please, do not let my tardiness interrupt your conversation."

"Philip was quizzing me about my arrival. It seems Mrs. Cobb has been bending his ear with dark hints about witchcraft and sorcery, since she still maintains she heard no cart, and neither did anyone in the village."

"Aunt Sibyl, you amaze me. Philip would not quiz." Amanda looked at him, warming his coattails at the roaring fire someone had thoughtfully provided this morning. "Philip would tell you not to talk childish nonsense. He would tell you that the so-called powers of witchcraft are nothing but the imaginings of a superstitious mind."

Philip held her gaze. Quietly, he said, *"Touché,* Amanda."

She inclined her head, noting that he looked rather pale. Perhaps the night had not been kind to him either.

He turned to his great-aunt. "Now, before I must brave the blustery morning, will you tell me at last why you came to see me here at Darring Court? You must have had a reason, for we both know you'd have enjoyed London much more."

"I had no choice. It was here or never. You see, my

dear boy, I don't know when I shall have another chance to look you up."

"So this is just another of your lightning-quick visits? Not the prodigal's return?"

"I shall be leaving before evening." She smiled. "My flying carpet is taking me on another journey. A very long one."

Philip looked as if he would protest, then thought better of it.

Sibyl said, "As to why I came . . . I wanted to meet your wife."

"You might have come to the wedding instead of sending a gift."

"Did you not like it?"

"A monstrosity." Philip grinned. "And it did not need a card to identify the giver. None other than my Aunt Sibyl would have presented a country vicar and his blushing bride with a gilded replica of an Eastern palace, complete with harem and dancing girls."

Amanda reached across the table for Sibyl's hand. "It is lovely. The squire offered a hundred guineas for it, but we declined. I use it in the dining room instead of an épergne, though Philip, if I don't watch him, tries to sneak it out when he has invited clerical friends."

Sibyl's silvery laughter rang out, and the frown that started to gather on Philip's brow never reached full ferocity. In fact, if it was possible that a handsome, distinguished looking gentleman could look sheepish, then that was the look that crossed Philip's face.

"You have my word," he told Amanda, "that I won't make the attempt again."

She scarcely heeded him but thought how tired he looked, his eyes shadowed and bleak.

No, she could keep the news from him no longer. She must tell him before the day was over.

He moved away from the fire. "Aunt Sibyl, now that

you have met and, I can tell, approved of Amanda, won't you stay awhile?"

"Please do." Amanda pressed the older woman's hand. "Your stamina and vigor may outstrip mine, but you cannot be looking forward to another journey so soon after your arrival. Even you must need a rest."

"Rest my old bones, you mean? And, indeed, I will. But not here. England is too cold for me. Philip!" Crooking an authoritative finger, she beckoned him close. "Your letters this past year have puzzled me greatly."

"Why? Did I not report succinctly on everything I undertook?"

"You started to sound like your grandfather."

Amanda stiffened. "Aunt Sibyl! That is hardly a compliment."

"It wasn't meant to be. And don't poker up, child. Philip understands me."

"I do, indeed." He had turned even paler. "It was a lecture of epic proportions, served in a nutshell. Will you excuse me, ladies?"

Sibyl reached out, took his hand and pressed it. "God bless you, my dear boy."

"You always said that at parting. Surely, you will be here when I return? I'm only seeing your friend, the warden, and should be back within the hour."

"Oh, yes. I should still be here. Let us say I took precautionary measures. At my stage of life, you take care to leave nothing unsaid. Nothing undone."

"Then, as a precautionary measure only—" Philip bent and kissed Sibyl's cheek. "Thank you."

"For what, my boy?"

"I am not quite sure yet. But by the time I return I should have worked it out."

He looked at Amanda. "Also, perhaps, when I return, we could have another talk?"

"But of course," she said faintly, the cup and saucer in her hand rattling so loud, the noise drowned the closing of the door behind Philip.

Five

Sibyl recommended that Amanda should see Philip in the study, the room he used exclusively when he visited Darring Court alone. And thus it was there Amanda directed her steps less than an hour after Philip had left. Preparing herself for a wait, she took with her a sewing basket and a half finished shirt. Not that she enjoyed sewing or counted it among her talents, but it was taught at Magdalen Home, and she believed she must set an example for the unfortunate women in the establishment.

Scarcely was she settled in a chair by the window, the shirt spread in her lap, when Philip strode into the room.

"Oh, good! You're early." Bundling the shirt, she tucked it back into the basket.

He joined her at the window. The ride had done him good. He no longer looked tired and drawn, only a little uncertain, which was quite unusual for Philip.

"You're not displeased that I am early?" He indicated the basket. "I am not disrupting your work?"

"Not at all. I just remembered that Miss Goodwyn wanted me to unpick every blessed tiny stitch I set last week."

"It seems the sewing mistress is a harsh task master. Whenever I see you with a shirt, you're unpicking what you sewed the day before."

"Not *a* shirt, Philip. *The* shirt. I began it two years ago when we opened the home."

Amusement glimmered in his eyes. "Then, perhaps, it is time to admit defeat?"

"Never." She drew a deep breath. "Philip, I shall be sewing more than ever. Not shirts but infants clothing."

"It is always best to master a small task before tackling a large one."

"No. I mean, yes, that is true, of course. But—"

"Amanda," he interrupted her quietly. "Forgive me, but I would like to speak to you on a different matter. Will you listen?"

She looked at him, once more aware that his usual air of self-assurance was missing. He seemed humble— yet how could that be when he had lost none of the power that could enthrall her with just a simple look, a very few words.

"Yes, of course I will listen, Philip. But I want you to know that I, too, have something of importance to say. You may go first, though. My news will still be the same, no matter when I tell it."

"You alarm me, but I shan't let you distract me now." Taking her hands, he drew her to her feet. "Amanda, I was such a fool—such a *pompous* fool to think that I must change you!"

Her eyes widened. "I agree."

His choke of wry laughter warmed her heart. "But what made you realize it, Philip?"

"Sibyl did."

"She spoke to you about me? About us?"

"She likened me to my grandfather."

"Oh. That. A lecture in a nutshell, as you called it."

"Precisely. And there were other things. It was seeing you with her. Hearing you talk with her." He touched an errant curl nestling against her forehead. "I don't want you changed. You're just the way I like you. The way you were when I fell in love with you."

Her heart was pounding. She thought she understood what he was telling her, but their past meeting had taught her wariness. Above all, she must stay composed. She turned a little, letting her gaze stray to the window. It faced south, the sea. The waves looked higher than the day before.

"Amanda? Am I too late? Can you not forgive me?"

She turned back to him. "Philip, I love you! I'd forgive you *anything.*"

He caught her in his arms. How she had missed the strength and warmth of those arms. The feeling of being loved and sheltered.

He said, "Then let us leave here. Immediately! We'll start anew. Together."

"But it's Halloween." Her protest was perfunctory and addressed to his chest, where her head fitted snugly. "We cannot leave before tomorrow."

"We can. Darring Court was my grandfather's obsession; it isn't mine. I have done my best to honor his wishes, but in truth, I think it is time to let go of this place. Amanda, I'll find another country parish. I vow, I'll make you happy again."

"A country parish?" She looked up in sudden misgiving. "Philip, what are you saying? Our home is in London. We have the schools . . . Magdalen Home."

"I will find someone to supervise them."

"But your work in London—Philip, you *told* me you no longer wanted to preach. You said the inheritance was God's gift that allows you to honor Him in a practical manner."

"I assure you, nothing we started in London will be neglected or abandoned."

She stared at him. "And your plans to sit in Parliament? To press for reforms—"

"I only want you." His embrace tightened. "I love you. I want to see you happy again."

"No! This is all wrong!"

"Why?"

She struggled against his hold, and with a puzzled frown he let her go.

"My love, why is it wrong what I propose?"

"It is pointless. A pointless sacrifice on your part. Your life is in London. And all I ever wanted was to be with you."

"We *shall* be together."

"But not where your life is. Your mission."

He was silent. After a moment, he started to pace.

"Philip, I am with child."

He stopped, his back to her, and stood stock still. Slowly, he turned.

"*What* did you say?"

"I am with child."

Indescribable joy lit his face. Mastering the distance between them in a single leap, he caught her around the waist. The next instant, she was lifted high and spun in a wild circle.

"A child!" he shouted. "You've made me the happiest man on earth."

Their eyes met, shared a moment of warmth, closeness.

She smiled. "And I believed I did that when I accepted your hand."

"You did." He slowed the spin, stopped, and carefully set her on her feet. "And now you did it again. Thank you, Amanda."

"Thank *you*, Philip," she said softly.

Cupping her face with his hands, he bent and kissed her. His mouth was warm. The taste of him, the scent of him, so achingly familiar, brought tears to her eyes, and their salty sting blended with the sweetness of his kiss.

Neither heeded the knock or the opening of the study door.

"A thousand pardons."

Amanda gave a start, her eyes drawn by the voice. A voice she detested, smooth as silk and, all too often, with the hint of a sneer. The voice belonging to the man she disliked above all others, the elegant Lord Knarsdale, who, alas, looked less than immaculate this morning in sea-spattered Hessian boots and pantaloons that were damp from the tops of the boots to his thighs.

He said, "My dear Darring, if I had known you were so pleasantly occupied, I would never have intruded. But no one warned me. Your housekeeper—but the least said about her, the better."

Philip released Amanda. "Knarsdale. I did not expect you. To what do we owe the pleasure?"

"Madam." The earl swept Amanda a bow before responding to Philip. "Good news, Darring. Fielding will be in town next week. A dinner at the club, a quiet talk, should do the trick."

Philip gave him an uncomprehending look.

"Fielding," Knarsdale repeated. "The justice, who may require a little wooing before he'll convince his nephew to withdraw."

Philip laughed. "You must forgive me if my mind is not on politics. Knarsdale, *I* have good news! You see before you the proudest, the happiest man on earth."

"But I have always known that, my friend." Again a bow to Amanda. "No man with such a beautiful wife could be less."

Her hands clenched, but Philip spared her the necessity of a reply.

He said, "Indeed, but now my cup runneth over, as the saying is. Knarsdale, I am about to become a father."

The earl's pale eyes narrowed as they swept Amanda's slender form. "My felicitations. And when, if I may inquire, will the happy event take place?"

"In truth, I forgot to ask." With a rueful grin, Philip turned to his wife. "My dear?"

"I should think in early June. Pray excuse me. You will have much to discuss about the upcoming election."

"Stay." Taking her hand, Philip raised it to his lips. "I will need you to be my counsel."

She searched his face. "Thank you, Philip. But you will do what is right."

Retrieving her sewing basket, she said, "My lord, we shall be pleased to have you join us for luncheon."

"You're very kind. Dare I ask that you extend your hospitality even further? I have a desire to join your husband in his watch over the bonfire."

Philip said, "You may take over the watch with my blessing. Amanda and I are thinking of leaving before nightfall."

"Leave!" A strange expression crossed Knarsdale's face. "You haven't forgotten the loss that would entail?"

Philip was about to reply when Sibyl, resplendent in a full-skirted gown of emerald-green wool, swept through the open door.

"What would my nephew lose, except a house for which he has no use? And why the show of concern, my lord? His loss would be your gain."

As Knarsdale greeted Sibyl, Amanda stood quite bewildered by the chair she had earlier occupied with her sewing. Whatever could be the meaning of their talk? She understood not a word, except that Philip still wanted to leave, only she hadn't the slightest notion whether that meant a return to London or a search for a country parish. But why would Knarsdale gain through Philip's loss?

Sibyl saw her thus and exclaimed, "My dear, you must

think we're talking in riddles. Philip! I've been meaning to speak to you about this. How could you leave the poor child ignorant? She did not even know about the bonfire!"

"It doesn't matter," said Amanda. "But I do confess some curiosity about how Lord Knarsdale fits into the picture."

"My dear madam," drawled the earl. "How I do admire your ability to come straight to the point."

"Thank you. But will *you?*"

He raised a brow. "Indeed, I will. My family name, you must be aware, is Raven. I hold the island."

"Raven Island. And I thought it was named after the bird!"

"You were mistaken, my dear Mrs. Darring." He stood by the fireplace, one shoulder propped against the mantel, his expression one of ennui. Only his eyes were alert, resting with disquieting speculation on Amanda. "If the stipulations of the late Mr. Darring's will are not met, Darring Court will go to the Raven family. But I shall leave it to your husband to tell the full story. And, perhaps, the *Contessa* will contribute. Particularly regarding the bonfire."

"I have explained about the bonfire," Sibyl said coldly. "And I no longer hold that title."

Later, when Amanda sought the quiet of her chamber after luncheon, she was still mulling over the confusing historical and legal details added by Philip and Sibyl. Too confusing, and of little interest to her if Philip was prepared to leave before the close of All Hallows Even. All that mattered was that he would lose Darring Court, a prospect she found most appealing.

Too unsettled to rest, Amanda started to pack her trunk. Low tide was in about four hours. If they were to leave, it would have to be then. But Philip was playing host to Knarsdale.

She stopped at a window. The mullioned panes were dull, and she could barely make out the balustrade of the outer gallery. Beyond the stone stretched indeterminable grayness that could be sky or sea. But she heard the wind, its howl much fiercer than the previous day.

"Amanda."

She spun, her spirits lifting at the sight of Philip.

"I did not hear you enter. Just listen to that horrid storm!"

"It's looking bad." He joined her, gathering her in his arms. "I fear the cart track to the mainland won't be passable today."

"But at low tide . . . ?"

He shook his head. "Cobb's cousin, the ferryman who brought Knarsdale, is still here. Would you brave a boat once more?"

She remembered the previous crossing, the tossing and pitching, the ice-cold spray dousing her, the waves so much higher and longer than the boat.

"I think not, Philip. Do you mind?"

"I want what is best for you and the baby."

"Let us stay on, then." She smiled faintly. "At least, in this storm you won't have to worry about the bonfire being lit tonight."

"You don't know the people here. They will try." His arms tightened around her. "But they may do as they please. It is no longer my concern."

She let her head rest against him. Much must yet be said between them, thanks to Knarsdale's untimely arrival. But for just a little while she wanted to savor this precious moment of peace in the midst of a storm.

At last she gathered the courage to face him. "When we do leave, where will we go?"

"Amanda—"

"My dears, I beg your pardon." Sibyl stood in the door. "But it is time I said good-bye."

Amanda deserted Philip. "I shan't let you go in such a storm. 'Tis madness, Aunt Sibyl!"

"Silly child." The old lady's voice was soft, but her hug was fierce. "I only regret that I did not make an effort to meet you sooner. Philip, my dear boy. Come and give me a kiss."

He bent and kissed the proffered cheek. "I know it's useless to try to make you change your mind. Farewell, dear aunt. And thank you!"

Her bright gaze darted from him to Amanda and back to him. "I cannot accept gratitude. Not yet. There are still shadows in Amanda's heart."

"I am aware of it." Philip hesitated. "But you of all people should know that the only way to eliminate all shadows is to walk alone in a desert. And even then, there's still your own."

Amanda's heart sank. This could only mean that he was still determined to retreat to the country.

Philip said, "If you're planning to leave with Cobb's cousin, Aunt Sibyl—"

"I am not. I still have a friend to see in the village. He will take me across."

Philip's brow darkened. "Your friend, the warden? Old Gregory is eighty if he is a day!"

"And I am seventy-eight. Are you saying that age makes us feeble?"

"Philip wouldn't," said Amanda. "He has too much discretion. And besides, he knows you have Abdul. Even that shapeless robe cannot hide the physique of a prize fighter. And since he attended Oxford, I should imagine he knows how to handle a boat."

Philip frowned. "You met the mysterious Abdul?"

"Yes." Amanda saw Sibyl staring at her. "Why, what is the matter, Aunt Sibyl?"

"You *saw* Abdul?"

"Indeed, he spoke to me."

Sibyl suddenly looked very old, very weary, the skin beneath the pink face powder ashen. She seemed to shrink into herself, her gaze withdrawn and shuttered.

Just as suddenly, her vigor revived. She turned to Philip. "My boy, you know the curse that plagues me. Do not waste time asking questions. Only take Amanda off this island. Immediately."

Six

Philip blanched. "Aunt Sibyl—"

"Go! There is no time to be lost."

He nodded, gripped Amanda's arm.

"Wait!" cried Amanda. "Will someone please explain?"

Propelling her by the shoulders, Philip said, "Sibyl has a gift—she calls it a curse—of foreseeing danger, a possible tragedy. When it became known, people called her a witch."

They were in the dark corridor and still Philip did not release his grip or slow the pace.

"We need a light," protested Amanda, and then Sibyl was there with a lantern.

"But why must I leave? Do we know what the danger is?" Amanda tried in vain to wriggle from Philip's grasp. "Philip, you're pushing. Stop. Have you considered? We can only leave in a boat! What could be more dangerous than a boat out in a storm?"

She felt Philip's hesitation, but Sibyl urged them on. "Hurry!" she cried. "The danger is here on the island. I don't know what it is, but I feel it!"

Amanda did not understand what was happening, but Sibyl's agitation was a palpable thing reaching out and spreading until Amanda felt it like a wave washing over her. Instinctively, she increased her pace. If there was danger, she would take no risk. She had a child to consider.

They found the kitchen dark and empty.

"Cobb's cousin must have left," said Philip.

Sibyl bundled Amanda in a heavy black cape from a peg by the yard door. "Hurry, and you may catch him before he casts off."

"This is madness." Philip was looking at the window above the sink. Rain poured against the panes, and gray daylight had turned to the black of night. "Aunt Sibyl, if I did not know you so well—"

"But you do." Sibyl handed him the lantern. "I shall seek out Gregory. His boat is small, but it could carry you both if the ferryman is gone. Only promise me, Philip—promise on the life of your unborn child that you will not linger or delay but make every effort to see Amanda safe."

Sibyl's eyes were wide and compelling, the agitation emanating from her making Amanda shiver.

"I promise," said Philip.

"Then go with God, my dear ones." And Sibyl opened the door and walked out into the storm.

"A cloak!" shouted Amanda, starting after her. The wind was so strong, it all but drove her back. "Aunt Sibyl, you don't have a cloak!"

Philip caught her. "She is gone. Take my hand before you stumble."

"She's there, going toward the park! Don't you see her with Abdul? The white robe, and—"

"Amanda, there is nothing to see. Come, we must go to the village."

She wiped the rain from her face. A moment ago she had seen the flutter of white; now it was gone. Still, she hesitated. "Philip, she *is* a very old lady. We shouldn't have let her go."

"She is *Sibyl*, my love. When she has set a course, no one can sway her from it."

"Darring!"

Amanda spun. She had quite forgotten about the Earl of Knarsdale, who stepped cloaked and booted from the kitchen. And, judging by Philip's groan, neither had he remembered their uninvited guest.

"I say, Darring! Is this fair? First you abandon me to your aunt. Then she disappears. There's no one to serve me. And now it looks as if you plan to desert me altogether."

"My apologies." Philip brushed a coat sleeve over his streaming face. "The Cobbs don't stay on the island on Halloween, and the help must have returned to the village. I am most awfully sorry, but you'll have to fend for yourself. This is your house now—or will be when the day is over. I am taking Amanda across."

"My dear fellow! Do you intend to swim?"

Amanda shivered and pressed close to Philip.

Giving her hand a comforting squeeze, he told Knarsdale, "I hope to catch the man who ferried you. Again, my apologies. I shall see you in town."

"Go if you must. But why drag your poor wife on what might be a fool's errand? Leave her until you've made certain the boat is still here."

"No." Amanda clutched her flapping cape. "I prefer to go with Philip. It would be precious time wasted if he had to come back to fetch me."

But Philip disagreed. "If you're here, at least you can detain old Gregory when he shows up. Who knows, but we may need him yet."

Giving her a quick, fierce hug, he pushed her toward the kitchen door.

"Much obliged, Knarsdale. Keep her safe for me."

* * *

At first the kitchen had seemed warm, a haven from the battling storm. But a quarter hour passed, and waiting became torture. Amanda paced the kitchen floor. Her gown beneath the wet cape was clammy, her hair was wet and cold and clung to her face, to her neck, because she had lost most of the pins. But she would not join Lord Knarsdale by the stove, where he had stoked the fire and made himself comfortable in Mrs. Cobb's rocking chair, a glass in his hand and a bottle, discovered in the pantry, on the floor beside him.

They had scarcely exchanged three words, but she was painfully aware of him, of those pale eyes following her every move. She stopped at the window but could see nothing, except that the rain had ceased. The wind still howled as fierce as ever, if not worse.

Do not delay, Sibyl had warned, and Philip was doing his best to obey. If only they knew where the danger lay. Nothing stirred outside, except for the wind. Then why the mounting anxiety, the trickle of sweat on her cold skin?

"Tell me, my dear Mrs. Darring," said Knarsdale. "Why did you attack me so fiercely at the Home Secretary's dinner?"

She turned slowly. "Attack you? My lord, you exaggerate. I merely pointed out that your philanthropic gestures are meaningless. That you should give more freely. And for the right reasons."

He drained his glass, refilled it, still never taking his eyes off her.

"I'll have you know, madam, that I contribute most generously, especially to your and your husband's charities."

"You are a hypocrite, my lord. You contribute a few pounds to our schools—"

"A few *hundred* pounds, madam."

"Yet you let your own children starve!"

He rose, making the chair rock jerkily. "I am a man, Mrs. Darring. Neither married, nor a saint. But as I told your husband, I have no other children than the boy I sponsored into Eton. The woman you met, lied."

"And you never lie, do you, my lord?"

"I gave my word."

"The word of a gentleman. Which is why Philip believed you. To him it is impossible—it is unthinkable that a gentleman's word could be an outright lie. But I am not so inhibited. I had no trouble believing that poor shadow of a woman. And I saw those children she spoke of! The spitting image of their father—if only they weren't so thin!"

The sudden silence in the room was more chilling than the gale outside.

"Indeed," he said softly, setting his glass on the white-scrubbed kitchen table. He came toward her. "And where precisely did you see the children?"

"In Seven Dials. But you need not bother to look for them there. I found a safer place."

"In your schools, of course."

"No. Philip would have noticed them."

And would have had another reason to find fault with her. A venture into the notorious slum was not something he would appreciate in his wife. And, foolishly perhaps, she had wanted to spare him. It would have shocked him deeply to learn of his friend's perfidy in such a sudden, drastic manner. But that was none of Knarsdale's business.

Again, silence stretched between them. And Knarsdale's eyes still rested on her.

He said, "There is no greater ill a man can suffer than a woman who is without discretion. There is something to that effect in the Bible, as I have pointed out to your poor husband."

"Why are you so set on stirring up trouble? From the

moment we met, you have tried to set Philip against me. Why?"

"I do not try to set him against you. It is your tongue you must blame."

"My tongue may be sharp, but it is truthful."

"It is a bane, madam. If you were a nobody, I daresay it would not matter to me. But you're the wife of Philip Darring, whom I proposed for a seat in the Commons. I introduced you to the highest circles of the ton, and you were well received. But when your conversation attracts more attention than mine or that of your husband, then you must be dealt with."

"You're mad!"

"But of course. There has been a mad streak in the Raven family for generations. Don't you know that?" He laughed softly. "Wasn't it explained to you why the bonfire is guarded?"

Suddenly more afraid than she had been when Sibyl's anxiety affected her, Amanda edged away from Knarsdale.

He said, "Seventy years ago, your husband's grandfather fell in love with my great-aunt. But she believed herself a vestal virgin or some such thing and wanted nothing to do with him. Or with any man, except the one who called himself the Druid."

Amanda's mouth was dry. "I don't believe you."

He shrugged. "Come to the bonfire, Mrs. Darring. I'll show you where she died. Set herself aflame as an offering to the Lord of the Dead."

"I'm not going anywhere, except with Philip."

His hand shot out, closed around her arm in a bruising grip. "Come. I will show you where she died."

She screamed.

The door burst open.

"Philip!"

He sprang at Knarsdale, knocking him against the

sink. "What the deuce d'you think you're doing, Knarsdale? Let go of my wife!"

"My dear fellow!" Releasing Amanda's arm, the earl pressed a hand to his hip, which had cracked against the stone sink. "I don't know what the deuce *you* think you're doing, but I was about to escort your wife to the bonfire."

Amanda clutched Philip's hand. "Let us go! For goodness' sake, just let us go! I'll swim to the mainland if I must."

"We have Gregory and his boat." Philip cast Knarsdale a dark look. "I have never known my wife to scream, and I want to know what happened. I'll hear your explanation when you return to town."

"He's in his cups," Amanda said quickly. "Please, Philip! Let's go!"

Knarsdale bowed. "My profound regrets, madam. And my apologies if I frightened you."

She inclined her head the merest fraction, then swept out, clutching the cape as once more she was caught in the wind's brutal assault. Strong, familiar arms closed around her, lifted her. She did not usually care to be carried like a child, but she did not protest, only hugged Philip's neck and made herself as light as possible.

Sheltered in Philip's arms, she was no longer afraid. In fact, her fear seemed foolish now and quite out of proportion to the event that had inspired it. Knarsdale had gripped her and told her to accompany him to the bonfire site. He was, indeed, a little mad. And drunk. That was all. But she was beginning to feel rather ill and wanted nothing more than to be gone from Darring Court and Raven Island.

When she saw the boat, however, a tiny nutshell with two sets of oars, her determination dwindled. It was tied to a landing stage of sorts and tossed about mercilessly by the choppy waters. She was given no time to protest.

Philip handed her to a white-haired old giant in oilskins, who had jumped into the boat the moment he caught sight of them. Then Philip boarded, and before she could blink, they were off, the two men at the oars, while she sat on the floor in a puddle of icy water, but held quite safely between Philip's knees.

"Wouldn't never have tried to cross!" shouted Gregory, bending to the oars. "Not in this weather and against the tide. But Miss Sibyl said I must. She's been havin' one of her spells."

"How is she?" Amanda shouted back. The boat pitched, and her stomach with it. Desperately, she clutched Philip's ankles for support. "I worried about her, without a cloak or anything."

"No need to fret about Miss Sibyl. She's a witch, don't you know?" Old Gregory's chuckle was carried off by the wind.

"Look!" said Philip. "The bonfire!"

The old man did not turn, but steadily plied the oars. Amanda craned her neck to see past his bulk. She could not see the island, only choppy sea. The boat pitched, and there, suddenly was a blood-red sky where Raven Island should be.

The boat veered and listed precariously.

"Steady, sir!" shouted Gregory. "We're close now, and the current's against us."

Amanda felt Philip hunch low behind her, felt his leg muscles tighten at her shoulders as he worked the oars harder and faster. She saw a wall of water rising up, threatening to break over them. She closed her eyes and started to pray when icy cold water drenched her. She prayed for safe deliverance from the clutches of a hostile sea, prayed for strength and endurance for the rowers, prayed for her unborn child, for Sibyl, for Philip, Gregory, and herself. She kept her eyes tightly closed when the boat smacked against something, when she heard shouts, when Philip lifted her in his arms. She did not open them until he set her down in a warm chamber at the Raven Inn, where they had left the carriage and horses upon their arrival.

She looked at Philip then, his face reddened from the wind and the sting of the sea, water dripping from his hair, from his clothing; and she looked at herself, the sodden skirt clinging icily to her limbs, the pool of water collecting at her feet. And she started to laugh. She all but hurled herself into Philip's arms, hugging him tightly. Without warning, laughter changed to tears and wild sobs.

Philip rocked her, stroked her damp hair, murmured soothingly until she calmed. He wiped her face with a sodden handkerchief from his sodden coat pocket.

"A bath," he said. "What you need is a hot bath. The landlord promised a tub and hot water immediately."

"Water again! Lud, Philip! If I didn't feel as if I'd fallen into a salt keg, I wouldn't step in a tub of water for all the riches in the world." She captured his hand, pressing it to her cheek. "Were we foolish, Philip? Risking our lives, our child—"

"No," he interrupted firmly. "Sibyl has never been wrong. When she senses danger, then it is so." He frowned. "Tell me about Knarsdale. What happened to make you scream?"

She did not answer immediately. She would never forget that moment of fear when Knarsdale gripped her arm, his soft laugh when he spoke of the bonfire's history. But it was only a memory; nothing she could not deal with when she saw him again.

"He was bosky, Philip. And, I think, a little mad. Did his great-aunt burn to death in a Halloween bonfire?"

"Yes. I should have told you, I suppose."

Philip hurried to the door someone battered with the heel of a shoe, or so it seemed. It was the innkeeper, armed with a copper tub and accompanied by various underlings lugging pitchers and towels.

"Thank you." Philip remained by the door, holding it open. "I'll ring if we need anything else."

Bowing, the innkeeper and his underlings withdrew. Philip closed and locked the door.

He looked at Amanda. "Will this do? Will it give us the privacy you said you miss?"

"It will do very well." She smiled mischievously. "That is, if you can assure me that you remember the part of lady's maid?"

"I'll do better than that. Come closer to the fire, and I will *show* you."

The following day, mid-morning, Amanda was waiting for Philip in the courtyard of the Raven Inn. The wind had calmed, and the sun struggled gamely to break through the clouds. Not a bad day for travel—if only Philip would return and they could get started. He had left over three hours ago to fetch their luggage. Surely, it could not take so very long to pick up two trunks.

Surely, he would not allow Lord Knarsdale to detain him.

Once more wrapped in the heavy black cape Sibyl had snatched off a hook in the Darring Court kitchen, Amanda paced up and down in the yard. She watched the chasing game of cloud shadows and sunshine on the cobbles and was reminded of the shadows in her heart. They, too, played chase with patches of sunshine. Vast patches of sunshine.

She could be so very happy . . . if only Philip did not think he must give up everything he had worked for in London. If only he weren't embarrassed by her outspokenness. She did have discretion; never betrayed a confidence. He must know that.

What was it her mother used to say? Life isn't all sunshine and roses. Indeed, life was sunshine and shadows. And, perhaps, that was as it should be.

Amanda was about to venture to the waterfront to look for the boat that would bring Philip from the island, when he strode through the gate.

She ran to meet him. "Where are the trunks?"

"Burned."

She stood speechless.

"The fire we saw from the boat wasn't the bonfire. At least, it wasn't only the bonfire, which they had trouble starting anyway since the wood was wet. But Knarsdale tried to stop them. They had been drinking mead to keep warm."

"They?" she asked faintly. Philip was not his usual, precise self.

"Those islanders and their visitors who celebrate the Celtic Samhain." Philip placed an arm around Amanda. "In truth, I could not get a clear report on what transpired. But, apparently, the celebrants were roused to anger and chased Knarsdale back to Darring Court. They all carried torches."

"Oh, no! They burned the house down?"

"Only the walls remain."

She was horrified, could scarcely speak. "Then *that* is what Sibyl foresaw. But where is she? And Knarsdale?"

"Knarsdale is still on the island. He is all right. Only his dignity has suffered."

"But Sibyl! Was she not there? Did she not come with you?"

His look was troubled. "Gregory said she left last night, as soon as he set out to help us. But he doesn't know who might have ferried her across. I suppose we shall have to wait for a letter from her."

Battling the ever ready tears, Amanda nodded.

"There is one piece of good fortune, and it should

be here by now. Aha!" Philip pointed to a boy with a hand cart passing through the gate. "It's a miracle, really, that it wasn't burned."

As the boy stopped beside them, Philip lifted a painting from the cart. The portrait of Sibyl as a young girl. A corner of the frame was charred, and the canvas showed a streak or two of soot. Otherwise it was unharmed.

Amanda saw the painting through a veil of tears. Red hair, green eyes, and a wicked propensity for mischief. The witch of Darring Court. And the witch winked at her.

"Since this is our only piece of luggage," said Philip, "let us see how quickly we can depart. We can make Berwick in an hour and purchase a toothbrush, perhaps even a shirt for me and a fresh handkerchief for you."

"Make it a dozen handkerchiefs. I seem to do nothing but weep these days."

With the painting under one arm and the other around Amanda's waist, Philip directed their steps to the stables, where he ordered the carriage to be readied immediately.

The innkeeper accepted Philip's word that payment would be forthcoming, and a short while later they rattled out of the courtyard. A horseman reined in to let the carriage pass.

"It's Roberts!" Amanda let the window down. "Roberts! Over here!"

Philip opened the panel behind the box and ordered the postboy to stop. A grinning, sharp-featured young man, whom Philip had caught breaking into the boys school two years earlier, appeared at the carriage window.

"Good morning, madam. Mr. Darring. Got something for you. Messenger brought it. From the Foreign

Office. Just like the package you had last month. So I reckoned you'd want it right away."

"Well, hand it over," said Philip. "Don't just gab about it."

"Aye, sir." After some digging in his saddlebags, Roberts produced a wrapped and sealed package about the size of a man's hand. "Are you on your way home, sir? I thought you meant to stay another three days."

"Yes, we're going home," Philip replied absently, staring at the package with a frown. He looked up. "Rest awhile at the inn. Then join us in Berwick. At the Swan."

Roberts took off, and Philip told the postboy to go on.

Amanda glanced at her husband. He still looked absentminded, staring at the package. But there was something that could wait no longer.

"Philip—before you open the package, will you please tell me where home is?"

He gave a slight start, looked at her.

"London, my love." He reached for her hand. "If you're willing."

"Yes! Oh, yes! But are you sure?"

"I am. You were right, you know. The work we began in London is my mission." He hesitated. "But I am having second thoughts about sitting in Parliament. I will withdraw, Amanda."

"Because of me?"

"No. Because I may not be the judge of character I thought I was." He smiled suddenly, a wide boyish smile. "And then again, this pompous fool may change his mind once more."

"I love you, Philip!"

"And I love you—and whoever it is that will join us in nine months."

She started to correct him, but his mouth closed over hers even before his arms enfolded her in a warm embrace, and it became quite irrelevant how many months it would be. Nothing mattered until a particularly nasty jolt of the carriage all but tumbled them off the seat, and something dropped on Amanda's foot.

She bent to pick up the package Roberts had brought and handed it to Philip.

A strange look crossed his face. "Amanda, this is from the Consulate in Cairo. Like the notification of Sibyl's death."

"Well, open it. I daresay it's to confess they made a mistake last time."

"A long confession, then. This package is quite thick."

Philip broke the seal. Inside the heavy paper wrapping was a letter and something bundled in baize cloth.

He scanned the letter. "The consul apologizes that an item belonging to the deceased Madame Sibyl—"

"What does he mean, *deceased!*" Amanda said indignantly.

"The deceased Madame Sibyl Petrowna, née Darring—"

"Petrowna?" asked Amanda.

"Her last husband was Russian. Now don't interrupt any more. Just listen. It says that the item was mistakenly retained in Cairo. The Consulate is sending it now. And this letter is dated . . . September 20. That is about when I received the first one."

They looked at each other, then at the baize-wrapped item.

"Open it," said Amanda.

Philip handed it to her. "You do it."

Amanda held it for a moment. She took a deep breath, then grasped a corner of the baize wrapping and shook.

Into her lap fell a ring set with a star sapphire of magnificent size and surrounded by seven large diamonds. Sibyl's ring. The ring, she had wanted Amanda to have.

Moonlight Masquerade

Joy Reed

One

Minnie Maxwell pointed excitedly to the window of the millinery shop.

"Oh, Susan, do look at that lovely bonnet," she exclaimed. "Mrs. Gresham must have just put it out today. I'm sure she had nothing so pretty in her window when we came through the village yesterday. Let's go into her shop and try it on."

Minnie's companion, Miss Susan Curtis, critically surveyed the bonnet, a cream-colored straw ornamented with cerulean blue ruffles and ribbons. "Yes, it's very pretty," she agreed, adding prosaically, "But you know we haven't any money to go buying bonnets, Minnie. You have only sixpence left after paying for your costume for the Squire's party tonight, and I just spent my last penny on that ring at Rudges'."

Minnie brushed these arguments aside with a wave of a kid-gloved hand. "It doesn't cost anything to look," she said. "Come on, let's go in and see if Mrs. Gresham will let us try it on."

She was already pushing open the door to the milliner's shop as she spoke. Susan was obliged to follow after, or be left standing alone on the sidewalk. As she entered the shop after her friend, she reflected once again that she had never seen Minnie's equal for audacity. She herself would never have dared to try on a two-

guinea bonnet when she had only sixpence in her reti-
cule. But Minnie dared do this and even more audacious
acts on occasion, as Susan had reason to know. Minnie's
mother had died a couple of years previously, and her
father, wishing to provide his daughter with some sub-
stitute for the maternal care she had lost, had recently
returned to the village where he himself had grown up
and where his own widowed mother still resided. Minnie
now lived with her grandmother, and it was old Mrs.
Maxwell who had seen that she was introduced to Roxbury society, including the society of Miss Susan Curtis.

Though very different in temperament, the two girls
had immediately become fast friends. By the time Minnie had been acquainted with Susan a week, she was
treating her as her closest friend and confidante. Susan
had come to know Minnie quite well in the months that
had passed since then, and though she had found Minnie's friendship now and then productive of embarrass-
ing consequences, she could not deny that it had done
a great deal to enliven her previously quiet and unevent-
ful existence.

It was not that Minnie was a bad girl. Even Mama
admitted that, although she often shook her head over
Minnie's conduct. "I do not doubt that Wilhelmina
means well, but she is altogether too impulsive," Mama
was wont to say severely, when Minnie's impetuosity had
landed her and Susan in some scrape. "She needs to
think before she acts, instead of blindly following her
impulses. And you need to think before you blindly follow after her, Susan. You are a year older than she, and
I have always thought you a sensible, intelligent girl,
which I am afraid Wilhelmina is not. If she has any idea
in her head beyond beaux and ballgowns, I've never
seen any sign of it."

Although Susan had stoutly protested this statement,
she had done so more as a matter of form than from

any real conviction of its injustice. It was a fact that Minnie's conversation did tend to center around the subjects of beaux and ballgowns, with perhaps an emphasis on the former. Mama, of course, thought such preoccupation unmaidenly.

"When I was a young girl, I can remember my mother scolding me for being forward, only because I once spoke to a gentleman who had not been formally introduced to me. No lady in my day would have dreamed of chasing after the gentlemen as Wilhelmina does. If she doesn't watch herself, I am afraid she will gain the reputation of being fast."

This statement, too, Susan had protested, though she herself had more than once marveled at Minnie's forward behavior toward the opposite sex. When they were out walking, Minnie thought nothing of boldly accosting any good-looking gentleman whom she happened to see on the street, and she had often hurried Susan down half-a-dozen blocks at a near run in order to arrange an "accidental" encounter. Mama said such behavior was calculated to give gentlemen a disgust, but Susan had observed that the opposite seemed to be true. At the monthly village assemblies, no young lady was more sought after as a partner than Minnie, and though she might be rather brazen sometimes about dropping her handkerchief, there always seemed to be plenty of cavaliers near at hand to pick it up.

In the beginning, Susan had been rather shocked by the freedom of her friend's manners. Hers was a loyal nature, however, and she stood by Minnie even when she herself could not approve of her conduct. Besides, once her initial shock was past, she discovered that there were advantages in being friends with such a girl. No matter how many gentlemen might beg Minnie to stand up with them, she could only dance with one at a time, and the overflow tended to pass naturally to Susan's lot.

In all the parties Susan had attended with Minnie during the past six months, she had never once been obliged to sit out a dance for lack of a partner.

This, of course, was a gratifying circumstance. But though Susan's partners generally seemed tolerably satisfied with their second choice, she found it a little galling never to be their first. Without being at all vain, or, she trusted, blinded by jealousy, she could not feel that her personal advantages were so greatly inferior to Minnie's.

She had at the moment a good opportunity for comparison, for she and Minnie were standing in front of a large plate-glass mirror which the milliner had provided for the convenience of customers trying on hats and bonnets. Minnie, beside her, was talking to the milliner, describing the bonnet in the window with animated gestures. She was of medium height with a pleasingly plump figure, a round dimpled face, long-lashed blue eyes, and curly blond hair cropped short. Altogether her appearance was very attractive. But was it not possible that some people might find a taller, slimmer girl with dark hair and gray eyes equally attractive? To Susan, surveying herself and her friend side by side in the glass, it seemed a not impossible idea. It would merely be a matter of personal taste as to which style of girl was preferred.

The milliner, having been made to understand Minnie's request, went to the front of the shop to bring in the bonnet from the window. Minnie turned to Susan with an ecstatic air. "Did you ever see so many pretty hats and bonnets? And Mrs. Gresham says she expects a new shipment from Paris any day now. I ought not to come in here, upon my word I ought not. Every time I do, I see half-a-dozen hats I simply can't live without. Oh, thank you, Mrs. Gresham—yes, that's exactly the one I mean. Do you think it will suit me? You're too kind—but upon my word, it does look well, doesn't it?

I can't see how I can ever bear to take the darling thing off, now I've seen it on me. Here, Susan, would you like to try it on, too?"

Susan assented and removed her own plum-colored Yeoman hat to try on the cream-colored straw. It looked well enough on her, though not so well as on Minnie, she was obliged to admit. A green plaid Huntley bonnet which the milliner produced from behind the counter was found to suit her much better. But as neither she not Minnie possessed enough money to buy either of these elegant *chapeaux,* they were obliged at last to remove them from their heads and return them to the milliner.

"Thank you so much for letting us try them on, Mrs. Gresham. I'm sure we've been a great deal of trouble to you, but I simply could not resist the urge to come in and see what that lovely cream-colored straw looked like on. And if I had not already spent my allowance, I should buy it in a trice: upon my honor, I should."

"You're very welcome, Miss Maxwell. No trouble at all," said the milliner. There was an indulgent smile on her face as she let Minnie and Susan out of the shop. People usually were indulgent where Minnie was concerned, Susan had noticed. No matter how troublesome her behavior, she had only to smile and beg their pardon to be excused in an instant. Susan was reflecting on this phenomenon with a mixture of envy and admiration when she was distracted by an excited cry from Minnie beside her.

"Susan, isn't that Harry DeForest over there in front of the stationer's? Yes, it *is* Harry, upon my word! Well, this is a surprise! I had no idea he was coming into the village today. To be sure, he *did* come to call on Grandmama yesterday, and I *did* just happen to mention while he was there that I was going shopping with you this afternoon. I daresay he had the idea of coming here, too, so he could meet me as if by accident. How very flattering, to be sure!"

"If you could be sure he did not merely come to buy stationery," said Susan, rather dryly. She had admired Harry DeForest for years before Minnie's arrival in the village, and it always annoyed her to hear Minnie talk as though Harry was her personal property. But though she disliked pandering to Minnie's vanity, she could not resist the urge to question her about the statement she had just made concerning Harry. "Do you mean to say that Mr. DeForest called upon your grandmother yesterday?" she inquired in a diffident voice.

"Yes, and he stayed nearly an hour. I don't believe he came just to gossip with Grandmama, either!" Minnie giggled and threw Susan an arch look. "He has been growing very particular in his attentions lately. Grandmama was remarking on it only last night. She quite put me to the blush, I assure you." Sinking her voice to a whisper, Minnie added, "Upon my word, Susan, I really believe he means to make me an offer. For the longest time I refused to credit it, for you know what a rattle Harry is. And then, of course, he is terribly eligible, too. I supposed his family would oblige him to marry some wealthy titled lady, or at least a lady with more of a name and fortune than mine. But I don't think there can be any doubt that he does mean to offer for me. Indeed, I wouldn't be surprised if he did it tonight at the squire's party. That's part of the reason why I've been so particular about my costume, you know."

"Indeed?" said Susan, with great restraint.

"Yes," said Minnie happily. She shot an assessing look toward the gentleman standing in front of the stationer's. "I don't think Harry's seen me yet. He's standing there talking to another gentleman—Mr. Sheffield, I think it is. I declare, I have half a mind to duck around the corner before he does see me. I am sure that if he does, he will only tease me some more about my costume for tonight. I told him yesterday that I wasn't about to give my secret away, but he simply would not leave the subject alone." Minnie giggled suddenly. "But there, perhaps he had his reasons for being so persistent. I suppose, as he means to propose to me, he wishes to make sure he proposes to the right lady!"

"Indeed," said Susan again, this time in a rather speculative voice. She too, shot an assessing look toward the gentleman standing in front of the stationer's shop.

Mr. Harry DeForest, at six-and-twenty years old, was indisputably the most eligible bachelor in the village of Roxbury. He was tall, well-built, and dashingly handsome, with light hair, a cleft chin, and a pair of laughing blue eyes. He was, moreover, the heir to a baronetcy, and was known to possess a considerable fortune in his own right. But as Minnie and Susan had frequently agreed, it was his air and address that set him head and shoulders above the other gentlemen in the village, even more than these other attractions. Harry could make a simple inquiry after one's health seem like the most flattering of addresses, and when he smiled and bowed gracefully over one's hand, one would have had to be insensible not to feel one's heart beat a little faster.

So Susan had felt, at least, on the occasions when she herself had been fortunate enough to receive Harry's addresses. But it was a mortifying fact that such occasions had been rare. Harry had always been perfectly friendly and polite to her, but then he was friendly and polite to everyone—that was part of his charm. He had certainly never distinguished her to the extent that he seemed to be distinguishing Minnie, if Minnie's reports were to be believed. Susan would rather have not believed them, but though Minnie was known to exaggerate on occasion, it was not like her to make up a story out of whole cloth. If she believed Harry to be about to make her an offer of marriage, then very likely he had given her good grounds for her belief.

This was a bitter pill for Susan to swallow. She had never seriously supposed Harry would ever make *her* an offer of marriage, but still she had allowed herself to dream that someday, somehow, such a thing might come to pass. She might not have blond curls and dimples, but she was still a pretty girl, and she felt confident that she was more intelligent, more accomplished, and possessed of a better-informed mind than the notably feather-headed Minnie. If only Harry would see and recognize her good qualities, surely he could not fail to be impressed by them!

But it was a lamentable fact that Harry had entirely failed to be impressed by what he had seen of Susan's qualities thus far. And for this he could not be held responsible, as Susan recognized with chagrin. It was her own awkward behavior that was to blame. Whereas Minnie was forward to the point of brazenness, she herself was unfortunately rather shy, so that on the rare occasions when Harry did address a few words to her, she was so tongue-tied that she could hardly stammer out two words together in reply.

There was only one occasion when she had managed to overcome her shyness in his company. At the Squire's All Hallows' Eve masquerade party the year before, she had flirted with a gentleman who had closely resembled Harry in height and features. Emboldened by the novelty of the situation and the circumstance of their both being masked, she had eventually permitted this gentleman to kiss her, a permission of which he had availed himself with enthusiasm.

Since the gentleman had been disguised at the time, and since Susan she had been obliged to leave the party before the unmasking took place, she could not be positive that it was Harry who had kissed her. But what other gentleman could have behaved with such a combination of wit, gallantry, and daring? Susan was quite sure it could have been no one else. Accordingly, she treasured the memory of that kiss as the most exciting and romantic moment of her life.

It seemed now, however, as though that moment was never to be repeated. It had taken place exactly a year ago, on All Hallows' Eve, and as was the Squire's invariable custom, a masquerade party was being held again that evening at Roxbury Old Place, the Squire's ancient and stately home. Susan had been looking forward to this party for some weeks with a more than ordinary interest. But if Harry were on the verge of offering for Minnie, he was unlikely to be dispensing kisses to other girls at the party. It was enough to make her consider forgoing the party altogether—or, if not quite that, at least to make her feel extremely downhearted.

Mama, of course, would say that she had been wrong in the first place to form such a decided partiality for Harry. It was Mama's opinion that a lady ought to keep her feelings for a gentleman rigidly in check and give him no encouragement at all until he had signified that his intentions were serious. Susan had abided docilely by these rules during the first eighteen years of her life, but of late she had begun to question their validity. She had no wish to appear an unladylike hoyden, openly pursuing first this gentlemen and then that in quest of a wedding ring, but at the same time she could not see that there was anything inherently unladylike about wanting love and romance and a home and family of one's own. Susan did want these things, and she was beginning to fear that unless she went out looking for them, they might escape her altogether.

This thought was in her mind now as she watched her friend's futile attempts to attract Harry's attention. Although Minnie had just assured Susan that she wished

to avoid him, Susan knew better than to take such as-
surances at face value. Minnie would sooner have deprived herself of food and drink than of a chance to
flirt with Harry, and when all her attempts to attract his
attention failed, she threw off all pretense of reluctance
and set off down the street to assail him in person. As
before, Susan was obliged to follow or be left standing
by herself.

When Susan arrived in front of the stationer's, she
found Minnie already deep in flirtation with her quarry.
"Oh, Harry, how can you tease me so?" she said, batting
her eyes at him in a manner that would have won Susan's
mother's instant condemnation. "I've already told you
that I am determined to keep my costume a secret from
everyone but Susan. You will simply have to wait until
tonight to see what it is."

"Now I call that cruel," said Harry, looking as though
he greatly enjoyed the game. "What if I don't recognize
you in your costume? Why, I might spend all evening
looking for you and not find you—and then I wouldn't
get a chance to dance a single dance with you. And in
that case, I might as well put a period to my existence
directly. It'd break my heart to go all evening without
dancing with you, Minnie, upon my soul it would. You
wouldn't want me to break my heart now, would you?"

"I don't believe you've any heart to break," said Minnie, tossing her head and throwing him a roguish look.

"Upon my word, I do. It's near to breaking right now
with the cruel way you've been treating me. Won't you
take pity on me, Miss Curtis?" he said, turning to Susan.
"Just whisper to me a word of what she'll be wearing
tonight, and I'll be your slave forever."

"Don't tell him, Susan!" squealed Minnie, clutching
Susan's arm in pretended alarm. "You mustn't tell him
a thing."

Susan, previously annoyed at being ignored, was now

embarrassed to find herself the center of attention. "I am afraid I am vowed to secrecy, Mr. DeForest," she said, trying to speak lightly. "You must not try to bribe me with offers of—of everlasting servitude. However, I doubt not you shall succeed in penetrating your incognita's disguise if you really apply yourself to the task."

Susan congratulated herself that she had achieved an admirably light and easy tone in making this speech, but it was evident that the word *incognita* was unfamiliar to Harry. "In discovering my what?" he demanded, looking at Susan in bemusement.

"Incognita," said the gentleman beside him, speaking for the first time. "From the Latin for 'unknown'."

"Ah, just so," agreed Harry, with a charming smile. "Imagine your knowing that, Miss Curtis. I never was much of a hand with Latin myself. Dashed clever of you." Having bestowed this encomium upon her, he turned again to Minnie and was soon embarked upon a confidential flirtation in which the words, "Really!" and "Oh, that is too bad of you, Harry. I shan't listen to another word, indeed I shan't," were frequently elicited from Minnie, along with fits of delighted giggles. Susan, finding herself excluded once more, had no choice but to turn to Harry's companion, who had likewise been excluded from the conversation.

She would have been bound to acknowledge his presence anyway, for he was a gentleman quite as well known to her as Harry himself. She had been acquainted with Richard Sheffield from the time they were both children. Their fathers' properties adjoined each other, and since their two families were on friendly terms, it was inevitable that their acquaintance should have continued up to the present day. Susan had always liked Richard well enough, and there was no denying that he had grown into a good-looking gentleman with the passage of time. Even Minnie, who would allow Harry to have

no serious rival in the neighborhood, was willing to con-
cede that Richard had slightly the advantage of the two
where height and figure were concerned.

"And of course he does have dark hair, and there's
something about dark men which is very romantic, I
always think. But Harry has such an air!" Minnie always
concluded the comparisons thus, with a rapturous sigh.
Susan quite agreed with her. In spite of a distinguished
Oxford career and two years spent serving under the
Duke of Wellington in the Spanish peninsula, Richard
had remained the same quiet, reserved gentleman he
had always been. His diffident, soft-spoken manner
could not compare with Harry's easy address and ready
wit, and all the romantic attractions of dark hair, broad
shoulders, and a good leg could not make up for it.

Susan was inwardly reflecting on this circumstance as
she smiled and bowed to Richard. "Good afternoon,
Richard. It's been an age since I've seen you in the village. Have you been visiting your cousins in London
again?"

"No, I have merely been busy about the estate," he
returned, with a civil bow. "My father's lumbago has
been very bad of late, and I have been obliged to take
over the work of running the property while he has been
laid up."

"Poor Mr. Sheffield! I am sorry to hear he has been
feeling poorly. Will his lumbago keep him from attending the Squire's party tonight?"

"I'm afraid so. He takes it very hard, I assure you. But
he has given me his blessing to attend without him,
which I count as a great boon." Richard hesitated a moment, then went on with some diffidence. "You and
your family will be attending the party, of course?"

"Not my family, no," said Susan. "It happens that
Papa was called out of town on business, and Mama does
not care to attend without him. Truth to tell, she has

no great opinion of the Squire's masquerades. I suppose they are rather sad romps, but great fun nonetheless."

"Perhaps she has taken her opinions from the rector's new curate," suggested Richard with a smile. "I understand that Mr. Nesbit has been begging Reverend Applewood ever since he got here for permission to preach against the impropriety of celebrating pagan festivals like All Hallows' Eve."

Susan laughed. "Poor Mr. Nesbit! He's doomed to disappointment in that endeavor, I'm afraid. Why, there's no one who enjoys the Squire's All Hallows' Eve parties more than Reverend Applewood. I overheard him talking to Mr. Nesbit last Sunday, after Mr. Nesbit had stopped some of the village women on their way out of church and told them they ought not to attend the Squire's party. 'Nobody denies that the day has pagan origins, Mr. N., but we're none of us pagans nowadays, I trust, and there's no sense setting people's backs up over a bit of harmless fun. When you've a parish of your own, you'll soon realize the wisdom of saving your sermons for the things that really matter, rather than wasting them on such trifles.' "

Richard joined in Susan's laughter at this speech and agreed that the curate's chances of converting the parish to his viewpoint were small. "If anything, I should suppose the Squire will have a larger attendance than usual tonight, for the weather couldn't be more perfect for an outdoor gathering," he added, with a glance at the blue and cloudless sky. "Of course, that need not weigh with those of us who are invited to the masquerade inside the house, but for the farmers and villagers who attend the bonfire party, it makes a big difference." With a touch of anxiety, he added, "You will be there, will you not, Susan? I hope your mother's disinclination to attend herself will not prevent you from coming?"

"No, for Minnie's grandmother has very kindly offered to take me with her and Minnie, and Mama said it would be all right," said Susan. She glanced at her friend as she spoke and observed with an inward sigh that Minnie was still deep in flirtation with Harry. Resigning herself to make conversation with her present companion for another half-hour, Susan turned again to Richard. "I am to dine and dress at Minnie's house before the party, and stay the night after," she told him. "Mama was quite relieved when Minnie's grandmother invited me to do so, for she had been worrying about my making the drive back to Longacre in the dark."

"I wish I had known that," said Richard. "I would have been happy to act as your escort, Susan—indeed, more than happy. If it ever happens again that I can serve you in such a way, I beg you won't hesitate to let me know."

He accompanied his words with another bow. Susan was surprised by his gallantry, but her attention was too much taken up in trying to overhear Harry and Minnie's conversation for her to wonder at it. She only smiled and shook her head.

"That's very kind of you, Richard, but though I'm grateful for the offer, truthfully I'm just as glad things worked out as they did. Even if you had escorted me to the party, I'm afraid Mama would have insisted on my leaving early. This year, I have hopes of staying until the party is actually over—or at least until after the unmasking. To my mind, more than half the fun of a masquerade is in the unmasking, and I was quite vexed to be obliged to miss it last year."

Susan stole a look at Harry as she spoke, wondering once again if he were the masked cavalier who had distinguished her so delightfully the previous year. She scarcely heard Richard's quiet rejoinder. "Yes, I was disappointed not to find you after the unmasking last year, Susan. I trust I shall have better luck this year."

Susan smiled and nodded, but her attention was once again with Minnie and Harry. It appeared from their conversation as though they were bringing their flirtation to a close. "No, there's not a bit of use teasing me further, Harry," Minnie was telling him, with a flutter of her eyelashes. "I've given you one hint, and that will have to serve, for I don't intend to say another word about it. I shall see you at the party tonight—and perhaps you shall see me, too, if you are clever enough to discover who I am! Good day to you, Harry—and good day to you, too, Mr. Sheffield. Forgive me for paying you no heed until now, but this sad rogue of a Harry has been teasing me to death about my costume for tonight. I really haven't had a chance to get a word in edgewise."

"No need to apologize, Miss Maxwell," said Richard with a smile and a bow. "Good day to you, and my best regards to your father and grandmother. And good day to you, too, Susan," he continued, bestowing another bow on Susan. "I trust I shall have the pleasure of dancing with both you and Miss Maxwell tonight, assuming I am intrepid enough to penetrate your disguises."

"Won't be any difficulty there, by Jove," said Harry, favoring both ladies with his dazzling smile. "We'll just have to look for the two prettiest girls in the room, eh, Sheffield?" Having reduced the two girls in question to smiles and blushes with these words, he finished them off with a killing bow, then set off down the street with Richard. Susan's response was very adequately summed up by Minnie's ecstatic whisper:

"Oh, Susan, I am simply wild about that man. He really does have the most divine air!"

Two

"Well, girls, we're here. Don't forget your fan there, Minnie—and Miss Curtis, mind you take care as you get out. Those steps are a bit steep."

Mrs. Maxwell delivered these instructions in a rich, smiling voice as she, Minnie, and Susan prepared to quit her carriage in the court before the Squire's house. The carriage was an old-fashioned coach, broad and heavy and comfortably upholstered, very much like Mrs. Maxwell herself. Minnie's grandmother was a fat, fresh-faced, jolly-looking old lady with blue eyes as bright and merry as her granddaughter's. Normally she wore her iron-gray hair tucked beneath a neat cap, but tonight it was dressed in ringlets and graced with a crown set with large, frankly false jewels. Her roly-poly figure was encased in a dress of stiff blue brocade worn over a quilted ivory satin petticoat. Mrs. Maxwell had chosen to attend the Squire's masquerade in the costume of Queen Anne. Susan, regarding her smilingly from across the carriage, thought to herself that it was a very appropriate costume. Old Mrs. Maxwell's fondness for brandy and water was almost as well-known as that of the monarch she was impersonating.

Minnie, beside her grandmother, was obediently obeying that lady's behest and gathering up her fan, shawl, and other appurtenances. Susan did the same, stealing a glance at her friend as she gathered together

her belongings. Minnie looked as unlike her normal self tonight as might well be imagined. Her plump figure was swathed in Eastern draperies of purple and gold, and her blond curls were entirely hidden beneath an elaborately dressed black wig surmounted by a gold turban. A sheer veil covered the lower part of her face, leaving only her eyes exposed. She had shamelessly darkened her lashes and brows, so that it was almost impossible to recognize her as the fair and thoroughly English-looking Wilhelmina Maxwell.

With a pang, Susan admitted to herself that her friend looked very fetching in this garb. Doubtfully she looked down at her own costume, wondering if it were completely overshadowed by Minnie's eastern splendor.

A glance reassured her, however, Her costume might not be so exotic as Minnie's, but in its own way it was quite as attractive. Susan had chosen to appear as a Spanish lady that evening in a décolleté dress of crimson and black. Her dark hair was caught up behind with a high comb and lace mantilla, and she had a large black lace fan behind which she might flirt mysteriously. To better carry out her assumed character, she had studied out a few phrases beforehand in a Spanish lexicon, so that she might more thoroughly confuse her friends and neighbors. She felt confident that no one was likely to recognize quiet Susan Curtis in the person of a dashing Spanish *señorita*.

The great question that was concerning her now was whether her costume would make the desired effect on Harry.

Masked or not, she knew she would never have the nerve to approach him openly, as Minnie did. She could only station herself where he was likely to see her and hope for the best. Her task was made more complicated by the fact that she had no idea what costume Harry would be wearing that evening. The gentleman who had kissed her last year had been wearing a domino and mask, which simple garb was far and away the most common disguise adopted by the gentlemen attending the Squire's parties. If Harry chose the same costume this year, it would be no easy task to pick him out among so many others.

This was a depressing reflection to Susan. But on further consideration, she found several circumstances that gave her hope. One was Harry's inimitable air and graceful carriage, which she felt must make him immediately recognizable no matter how he might be costumed. Another was the fact that Minnie's Eastern draperies were such a thoroughgoing disguise.

Unless Minnie purposely did something to betray herself—unlikely, considering the mystery she had been studiously building up around her appearance—Harry was unlikely to recognize her without a good deal of searching. In the process of his search, it was probable that he would run across Susan. If she used her fan to any effect at all, Susan felt certain he must ask her to dance with him, for he was not a man to forgo the pleasure of dancing merely because he could not locate one particular lady among the crowd. That would be her chance—perhaps her last chance—to show him what he had been missing all these years in ignoring the charms of Miss Susan Curtis.

The idea that so much was riding upon this evening made Susan feel slightly nervous as she followed Mrs. Maxwell and Minnie down the steps of the carriage and across the drive to the Squire's house.

This was a large and picturesque structure built of brick and flint, dating from the late fifteenth century and known in consequence by the homely appellation of Roxbury Old Place. Susan, having lived all her life in the village of Roxbury, had visited the Squire's home numerous times, but Minnie had never before had occasion to set foot in the Old Place. As a pair of liveried and bewigged footmen admitted their party into the house's great hall, she looked around her with an expression that was at once eager, curious, and slightly critical.

"My, it's even bigger inside than it looks from the outside, isn't it?" she whispered to Susan. "I never saw such an enormous hall before. And look at that staircase! One might drive Grandmama's coach up it and have room to spare. But it's all rather shabby, isn't it? Why doesn't the Squire get some real furniture instead of all these ugly old tables and benches?"

Susan, who along with most locals was accustomed to regard the Squire and his property with a nearly feudal reverence, was rather shocked by this speech. But a moment's reflection reminded her that Minnie was a newcomer to the area and thus ignorant of all that was conveyed by the name of Roxbury Old Place. So she merely smiled indulgently at her friend and whispered back, "I suppose it *is* a bit shabby, but you know everything here is very old, Minnie. The Squire says this hall is exactly as it was in his great-grandfather's time. And if his great-grandfather hadn't found it necessary to replace some of the timbers in the ceiling, it would be exactly the same as it was when the hall was built back in the reign of Henry the Seventh."

"It looks it, upon my word," whispered Minnie with an irreverent giggle. Nonetheless, it was evident that Susan's speech had impressed her. She cast a respectful look at the hammer-beam ceiling high above them as they passed through the hall and out the door at its far end.

This door admitted them to an anteroom, where they joined a stream of other guests in fancy dress who were moving slowly toward the double doors that opened into the house's courtyard. Just outside in the courtyard, a

costumed gentleman who was unmistakably the Squire
was greeting his guests in his usual jovial manner.

The Squire was a small, wiry man, still young and energetic enough to be described as middle-aged but approaching that time of life when he must inevitably be
known as elderly. He had a face like tanned leather and
a manner that was at once brisk and expansive. For his
costume that evening, he had chosen to appear as a
rustic laborer in boots, smock, and breeches. He might
almost have been mistaken for one of his own husband-
men in this dress, had it not been for the air of authority
that enveloped him like an invisible cloak.

"Now lads, you'll find yourself more at home on the
terrace," he was saying in a voice both kind and firm,
as Susan, Minnie, and Mrs. Maxwell approached him.
"You be off around back and get yourselves a glass of
good ale, hey?"

The persons he was addressing, a couple of hulking
young countrymen whose dominoes imperfectly concealed their corduroy coats and stout boots, nodded
shamefacedly and turned away. The Squire's All Hallows' Eve party was really two parties, a bonfire party on
the terrace for the benefit of the villagers and local farming folk, and a more select party in the courtyard for
the local gentry. No specific invitations were issued, and
indeed there tended to be a certain amount of mixing
between the two groups, especially as the evening wore
on. It was not uncommon to see a farmer's wife with
social aspirations gravitating toward the party in the
courtyard, or a gentleman who preferred strong ale to
champagne rubbing shoulders with his tenants around
the bonfire. For the most part, the Squire was content
to stand back and let everyone find his or her own level,
but now and again he found it necessary to step in and
address a word to some especially flagrant offender, as
on the present occasion.

For Susan, Minnie, and Mrs. Maxwell, however, he had nothing but smiles and the warmest of greetings. "Ah, if it isn't Brandy Nan," he exclaimed, hailing Mrs. Maxwell with a mock-reverent salute. "Your Majesty won't find your favorite tipple at the refreshment table, but there's a drop of Fine Old Cognac somewhere hereabouts, I daresay. It's to be feared there wasn't no duty to the Crown paid on it, but Your Majesty'll wink at that this once, I hope!" He let one of his own eyelids droop in a sly wink. "Perhaps you'd be good enough to join me in a glass later on?"

"Don't mind if I do, sir," returned Mrs. Maxwell, with a rolling chuckle. "You just look me up when you're ready, and I'll join you in a glass with a right good will!"

The Squire promised to look her up as soon as he was at leisure, then turned his attention to Minnie and Susan. Minnie he stared at very hard, observing that it was difficult to say who she might be behind her veil, but that he had no doubt she was a rare beauty. Susan he likewise hailed as a beauty and, having kissed her hand in a gallant manner, inquired where she hailed from.

"But from Madrid of course, *señor,*" said Susan, batting her eyes at him behind her fan. "And you do me too much honor, I protest. We have many gallant gentlemen in Madrid, but none so gallant as you, I think."

The Squire, vastly pleased by this address, vowed to dance with both her and Minnie later on, then turned his attention to new guests who had just come into the courtyard. Susan, Minnie, and Mrs. Maxwell were thus free to mingle with the other merrymakers who thronged the square, stone-flagged pavement.

"You cannot call this shabby at least, Minnie," whispered Susan with a smile. "A bit rustic, perhaps, but it seems to me the perfect setting for an All Hallows' Eve party."

"Yes, indeed," said Minnie, looking around her with a delighted expression. The courtyard was bordered on three sides by the high stone walls of Roxbury Old Place and on the fourth by a stone wall pierced by a broad iron gate. Through the gate could be glimpsed the light of the bonfire on the terrace beyond, with the villagers and farming folk making merry around it.

The space within the courtyard was lit by innumerable torches that cast a flickering light over the costumed crowd. Heaps of garden produce and shocks of grain stood here and there, and a table in one corner of the courtyard bore such light refreshments as punch and sandwiches. More substantial fare was provided in the great formal saloon inside the house. In inclement weather the Squire was accustomed to hold his masquerades in this saloon, but Susan was thankful to see that such measures would be unnecessary tonight. It was a perfect evening for an outdoor party, clear, calm and only slightly cool. In her opinion, the Squire's parties lost a good deal of their rustic charm by being moved indoors.

While she and Minnie were admiring the picturesque scene around them, Mrs. Maxwell had found a vacant bench and sunk down upon it with a sigh of relief. "Well, girls, I don't mind saying I'm glad to get off my feet for a bit," she said. "But you'll be wanting to do a bit of dancing, I don't doubt. You ought not to have any trouble finding partners, as fetching as you both look tonight. Ah, here's a gentleman who's got an eye in his head," she said, beaming upon a masked dragoon who had just come up to join them. " 'Pon my soul, sir, you won't find two prettier girls if you look all night."

"I believe you, ma'am," he returned, with a gallant bow. "And if one of the young ladies will consent to partner me in this next dance, I should count myself very much honored."

It was Harry! There was no mistaking that graceful bow or that familiar, laughing voice. Susan was electrified to see that her chance had come so soon. Unfortunately, shock held her motionless a second, and this hesitation proved fatal. With a pretty air of timidity, Minnie stepped forward and curtsied deeply to Harry, batting her kohl-blackened lashes at him as she spoke.

"My friend and I thank you for the compliment, sir," she said. "I cannot speak for her, but for myself I should be very happy to dance with you."

Susan could have wept with chagrin. It was inconceivable that Harry would not recognize Minnie now. Even if by some miracle he had not yet tumbled to her identity, his state of ignorance could not possibly continue throughout the space of a whole dance. Susan's chagrin was but little lessened when, having tucked Minnie's arm beneath his, Harry turned to bestow a smiling bow on her.

"As for you, ma'am, I shall hope to have the pleasure of dancing with you later," he said. "I trust you're not booked for the whole evening?"

"By no means, *señor. Muchas gracias,*" said Susan, trying to smile, but feeling she would rather weep.

She watched gloomily as Harry and Minnie joined the line of dancers that was forming along one side of the courtyard. It was depressing to be left on the sidelines without a partner, and more depressing still to watch Minnie flirting gaily with Harry. Even when a gentleman presently approached Susan and invited her to stand up with him, her gloom was but little abated. In spite of his mask and watchman's costume, she had no trouble recognizing her would-be partner as Billy Babcock, a local young gentleman who was only a few years beyond adolescence and who still possessed the distinguishing characteristics of that period: namely, a gangling build, a bad complexion, and a loud and obnoxious manner.

"By Jove, but you're a pretty gal," he said, looking first at Susan's face and then at her décolletage in a manner she found extremely offensive. "Don't believe I've seen you around here before. You ain't one of the Potter girls from over at Netley, by any chance?"

"No, I know not where Netley may be. I come from Madrid," said Susan, rather half-heartedly reassuming her Spanish character. "Assuredly you would not have seen me before, *señor.*"

"What's that you say?" said Billy, regarding her with fascination. "Was that Spanish you was speaking? Say it again, so I can hear it better."

Susan was obliged to repeat her remark. *"Señor,"* repeated Billy with heavy emphasis. "Sounds Spanish, all right. By Jove, you really are from Madrid, ain't you? What's your name?"

"Rosa, *señor,"* said Susan, choosing a Spanish-sounding name at random. She was beginning to be sorry that she had entered upon her impersonation in Billy's company. She was also beginning to be sorry that she had allowed Minnie to talk her into removing the black lace ruffle that had originally filled in the low neckline of her dress. The way Billy kept looking at her chest made her want to hit him.

"Rosa, eh? That's a pretty name—a pretty name for a pretty lady. How long are you staying here in England, ma'am?"

"I'm sorry, *señor.* My English is very bad—I do not understand what you say," said Susan, taking refuge in her supposed foreignness in an effort to put an end to the conversation. By repeating the same words to every subsequent remark Billy made, she trusted he would soon tire of her company and would take himself off when the dance was over. But this did not prove to be the case. Billy, though clearly frustrated, seemed more intrigued than ever by her character and immediately invited her to stand up with him a second time.

"I'm sorry. I do not understand, *señor*," said Susan, smiling and edging away from him. In doing so, she nearly collided with a tall gentleman in a black domino who had come up to where she and Billy were standing. This gentleman made her a courteous bow.

"I beg your pardon, ma'am. I trust I'm not intruding, but I hoped you might consent to dance this next set with me if you're not already engaged."

"Oh, yes, I should be very glad to dance with you," said Susan fervently. She then remembered her character and added belatedly, *"Muchas gracias, señor."*

The tall gentleman smiled and bowed again, but Billy, who had observed this whole exchange, stiffened with indignation. "She can't dance with you. She's already booked to me," he told the tall gentleman belligerently.

"I am not," said Susan, nimbly taking refuge behind the tall gentleman's stalwart form. He gave her a look of surprised amusement, then turned to look at Billy.

"You seem to be mistaken, sir," he said politely. "The lady says there is no engagement between you."

"Yes, there is," insisted Billy stubbornly. "I asked her to stand up with me again the minute the first dance was over."

"And did she consent?" inquired the tall gentleman. His voice was very solemn, but Susan thought she detected a quiver of laughter in it.

Billy scowled. "No, she didn't consent exactly. But damme, that's only because she don't speak English worth a rap. I asked her all right and tight, and now I'll thank you to stand aside, fellow, and let us be off."

The tall gentleman looked at Susan. She shook her head vehemently. "I did not agree to dance with him," she whispered. "Upon my word, I did not!"

"I'm sorry, sir, but the lady insists she is not engaged

to you," he told Billy. "That being the case, I think you had better stand aside yourself and let us take the floor."

"I'm damned if I will," said Billy. "By God, this is an infamous business. I asked her first, and if you don't stand aside, I'll give you a taste of home-brewed you won't soon forget!" Putting up his fists, he brandished them toward the tall gentleman in a menacing manner.

In spite of her annoyance, Susan could hardly keep from laughing. The sight of gangling Billy Babcock threatening a gentleman so very much larger than himself was ludicrous in the extreme. The tall gentleman was obviously having trouble keeping a straight face, too, but when he spoke again, his voice was pacific. "Sir, I can understand your vexation, for anyone would regret losing a dance with such a lovely lady. But she insists she is not engaged to you and has, in fact, consented to dance this next dance with me. Surely you don't wish to cause her any embarrassment by contesting the matter so publicly?"

"I don't want to cause her any embarrassment, but I'm damned if I'm going to stand back and let her dance with anyone else when she's promised to me," said Billy stubbornly. "As far as I can see, it's you that's causing the scene by pushing yourself in where you ain't wanted. You can either take yourself off this minute, or get ready to have your cork drawn." Once more he brandished his fists toward the tall gentleman.

This action, combined with the loud voice in which Billy had spoken, had attracted the attention of some of the other guests. Susan saw heads turning in their direction and curious looks directed at her and her two companions. The tall gentleman appeared displeased by this publicity, but still he endeavored to pacify Billy.

"Indeed, I cannot think this an appropriate place to settle a quarrel, sir. If you really wish to meet me, I would be happy to do so, at any time and place you would consider convenient—"

"This place right now is convenient as far as I'm concerned," said Billy boastfully. The attention he was receiving from those around him was obviously having an intoxicating effect on him. He brandished his fists more boldly than ever as he went on tauntingly. "Don't say you're afraid to come to cuffs with me, fellow? A touch of the craven, eh?"

"Not at all. If we were alone, I would ask nothing better than the chance to pound some manners into you," said the tall gentleman calmly. "But at the present moment we are not alone. There is a lady present—a number of ladies, in fact—and as we are guests in someone else's home—"

"I don't care for that if you don't," interrupted Billy. "Put up your mawlies, fellow, or else take yourself off; it's your choice."

With a resigned but resolute air, the tall gentleman put up his fists and prepared to engage with Billy. A crowd at once formed around them. One or two gentlemen began crying excitedly, "A mill! A mill!" But before the tall gentleman and Billy could do more than exchange a few experimental jabs, the Squire came bustling through the crowd.

"Here, here, what's this?" he said, looking severely at the two combatants. "Don't either of you have any more sense than to start a row in front of the ladies?"

Both gentlemen looked guilty, but Billy, in a blustering voice, at once began to defend his actions to the Squire. "It was all his fault, sir. He stole my partner," said Billy, shooting a hostile look at the tall gentleman. "She was promised to me, by God, and I was damned— pardon me, sir, dashed—if I'd stand by and let him walk off with her without putting up a fight."

"The lady denies there being such a promise between

you," said the tall gentleman, returning his look with one almost equally hostile. "And as she *did* promise to dance with me, I had no choice but to defend my right in the matter."

The severity of the Squire's expression had greatly lessened during this speech. By the end of it, he was chuckling openly. The other guests around him began to laugh, too, and the mood of the gathering became suddenly much less tense. "Ah, so it's a lady you're fighting over, is it?" said the Squire. "I ought to have guessed as much. It takes a lady to throw a couple of young bucks like you into a pother. Who is this lady you're fighting over?"

Both Billy and the tall gentleman looked at Susan. "Her," said Billy concisely. The Squire grinned.

"Ah, it's you, is it, ma'am?" he said, addressing Susan. "I might have known you'd caused the mischief." To the two young gentlemen he said, "I don't blame you lads for quarreling over such a prize, but you know I can't have the pair of you brawling about underfoot and upsetting my company. We'll settle this in a civilized manner, if you please." Beckoning one of his servants to his side, the Squire issued some low-voiced instructions. The servant bowed, left the courtyard, and returned a few minutes later bearing a pair of button-tipped foils. The Squire took these from him and presented one to Billy and the other to the tall gentleman.

"There you go, lads. If you want to fight, you can do it this way, with no bloodshed," he told them. "Swordplay's the way gentlemen used to settle questions of honor in my day, and to my mind there still ain't a better one. Let's see you step lively now, and whichever of you breaks through the other's guard shall have the lady's hand for the next dance."

"I don't care for fencing," objected Billy, sulkily inspecting the foil. "Nobody does nowadays, sir. It's pistols that are the thing: pistols or fisticuffs. Why can't we have a shooting match to settle it instead?"

"You can't have a shooting match with ladies about," the Squire told him sternly. "Fencing may be a bit out of fashion, as you say, but you young blades would do well to study it all the same. It takes a deal more finesse to score a point fencing than to pull a trigger at a target, I can tell you that. Just you take up that foil, young master jackanapes, and let's have no more argle-bargle about it. Unless you'd rather the other gentleman won the lady by default?"

In front of so many witnesses, Billy could not consent to such a proceeding, but put up his foil with a sullen air. The tall gentleman, who had been critically examining his own weapon, at once did the same. The Squire took Susan by the hand and led her to the raised platform where the fiddlers were stationed.

"You stand here, ma'am, so they can see the prize they're fighting for," he told her with a grin. "I'll stand with you and act as judge. All right, lads, have at it. I want a good, clean fight, and whichever of you comes out the winner shall have the honor of leading off the next dance with the lady as his partner."

Susan, standing on the platform, blushed a little to find herself the cynosure of all eyes, but at the same time she could not help feeling rather gratified. Even if one of the contestants was Billy Babcock, it was still very exciting and romantic to have a pair of gentlemen fighting for the privilege of partnering one in the dance. She watched with interest as Billy and the tall gentleman lunged and parried and circled each other warily below on the court. She knew too little about fencing to be any judge of what was going on, but the Squire beside her watched it all critically and kept up a running commentary on the action.

"There's a clever bit of work," he would say approv-

ingly, when one of the opponents distinguished himself
with a deft piece of swordplay. More often, however, he
would exclaim, "Faugh! Clumsy!" with a shake of his
head. Now and then he called out impatiently, "Look
to your guard, man! Look to your guard!"

These words were addressed more often than not to
Billy, and indeed, it was clear almost from the beginning
that Billy was in difficulties. The tall gentleman fought
cautiously, without any display of virtuosity, but his play
was solid, and he had the advantage of Billy both in
reach and temperament. When Billy, in a fit of pique,
made a wild lunge for his opponent's heart, the tall gentleman neatly parried the blow and retaliated with one
that sent Billy's foil clattering to the pavement.

The Squire, beaming from ear to ear, leaped down
from the platform and grasped the tall gentleman by
the hand. "Well done, sir! Well done! Not but what I've
seen better swordplay in my time, if you'll pardon me
for saying so. Why, if I were twenty years younger, I'd
have a try for the lady myself—aye, and be pretty sure
of winning her, too!"

"I don't doubt it, sir," said the tall gentleman, smiling.
"I can only be glad I am spared such a formidable opponent."

The Squire, looking pleased, slapped the tall gentleman on the back. "Well, well, I don't say you haven't
reason to say so, but you've the makings of a pretty
swordsman yourself if only you'd apply yourself to it
regular. And you, too, sir," he added, looking kindly at
Billy. "Anytime you'd like to come over and put in an
hour with the foils, I'd be glad to oblige you. That was
a neat thrust in quatro you made there toward the end."

"I very nearly did pink him, didn't I?" said Billy,
brightening somewhat. Fortified by this reflection, he
consented quite amicably to shake hands with the tall

gentleman and promised to call on the Squire the following week for a session with the foils.

This business concluded, the Squire took the tall gentleman's arm and led him to the platform where Susan was standing. "There's your prize, sir," he said, ceremoniously placing Susan's hand in the tall gentleman's. There was a burst of applause from the audience, and several gentlemen cheered; the cheers and applause grew even louder when the tall gentleman carried Susan's hand to his lips, Susan felt she was blushing, but there was a happy glow in her heart as she stepped down from the platform and took her place opposite the tall gentleman at the top of the dance floor.

Three

As soon as Susan and the tall gentleman had taken their places on the floor, the fiddlers struck up a rollicking country dance. There was a scramble among the other guests to take their places in the line. Susan and the tall gentleman led off, and for the first few minutes neither of them spoke. When they had successfully gone down the line, however, and had retired to a place lower on the floor, the tall gentleman cleared his throat and addressed Susan in an apologetic voice.

"Forgive me for being such a dull partner," he said. "Truth to tell, it's taken me a minute or two to catch my breath after that little athletic exercise the Squire just put me through. I was afraid if I tried to speak *and* dance, while I was still so winded, I might disgrace myself by fainting away in your arms as we were going down the line."

Susan could not help laughing at the idea of such a brawny gentleman wilting away on the dance floor like a vaporish damsel. "That *would* tend to dilute your triumph a bit, wouldn't it?" she said. "Only think what the Squire would say! I expect he would shake his head and declare that in his day, young gentlemen could endure a trifling bit of exertion without coming over faint."

"I expect he would," said the tall gentleman, grinning. "I can almost hear him saying it now. I wonder if young gentlemen in his day were really such doughty characters as he remembers, or if his memory misleads him?"

"The latter, I suspect, but it wouldn't do to disillusion him," said Susan, throwing an affectionate look toward the Squire's smock-clad figure. "Perhaps he only remembers how he himself was. Papa says he was a famous sportsman in his day."

The tall gentleman nodded. "I can well believe it. He still sets a splitting pace in the hunting field." With a smile, he added, "But I trust he will set me no more athletic ordeals this evening. I want to sit back now and enjoy the fruits of my labor."

Susan gave him a deprecating smile. "I'm sorry that you were obliged to labor so hard on my account," she said. "It's infamous that you should have to wear yourself out rescuing me from Bill—from my other partner, that is. But I do appreciate your efforts on my behalf."

"It was nothing," said the tall gentleman, looking modest.

"Indeed, it was *not* nothing," said Susan warmly. "It was very generous of you to champion me as you did, and I assure you that I am extremely grateful for it. I only wish there was something I could do for you in return."

The tall gentleman looked down at Susan meditatively. "Do you?" he said. "That might be arranged, you know."

The way his eyes dwelt on Susan's lips told her exactly what kind of arrangement he had in mind. Once more she felt the color rise to her cheeks, but mingled with her embarrassment was a sense of rising excitement. This gentleman flirted quite as delightfully as Harry, and appeared to be quite as good-looking as Harry, too, from what she could see of him beneath his mask and domino. Had not Harry already been accounted for in another dress, she might have been deceived into thinking this was he. Susan studied the tall gentleman curiously, wondering who he might be. His voice was not familiar, but something in his manner of speaking made her suspect he was making a deliberate effort to disguise it. This reminded her that she, too, ought to be making an effort to disguise herself. Raising her fan to her face, she batted her eyes at her partner in a flirtatious manner.

"I know exactly what you mean, *señor,* and you are very wicked to say so," she told him with mock severity. *"En verdad,* it is too bad of you to embarrass me in such a way."

The tall gentleman's eyes gleamed through the slits in his mask. "Alas, *señorita,* you wrong me," he said, and to Susan's dismay launched into a voluble flood of Spanish in which she recognized not one word. Ruefully, she told herself that she should have chosen some other character to impersonate that evening—a French or Italian woman, perhaps. At least she could carry on a conversation in those two languages. Her Spanish impersonation had thus far brought her nothing but embarrassment.

The tall gentleman had finished his speech and was regarding her expectantly, as though awaiting a reply. "A thousand pardons, *señor,* but it has been many years since I left my native Spain," she told him, with as much dignity as she could muster. "I am afraid I do not comprehend what you were saying."

The tall gentleman's smile broadened into a grin. "Alas, that so much eloquence should be wasted! But I have no objection to repeating my words in English. I said you looked beautiful this evening, and that I felt privileged to be dancing with the loveliest lady in the room. Even if I had to fight a duel for the privilege!"

"Oh," was all Susan could think to say. Rather belatedly she added, *"Muchas gracias, señor."*

"De nada, señorita," he returned, throwing Susan into dismay once more. He considerately translated these words in his next speech, however. "That's to say you're very welcome, ma'am. And so you are, upon my word. I hope you don't think that in saying such things I'm merely paying you—Spanish coin." He threw Susan a laughing look. "You do indeed look very lovely this evening, and I'm not at all surprised your other admirer was so loath to give you up."

In spite of her renewed embarrassment, Susan could not help laughing. "Billy is such an idiot," she said. "Imagine, he thought I really was from Madrid, only because I called him *'señor'* and spoke a few words in Spanish! Whereas you saw through my imposture in the first five minutes." She gave the gentleman a shy smile.

He smiled back at her. "Billy isn't what you could call needle-witted, certainly, but he really isn't a bad sort. Like most boys his age, he's a bit resty and inclined to take snuff at imaginary insults. Time should take care of that, however, and I trust he may already have learned the unwisdom of starting a brawl at an evening party!"

Susan took note of this speech, which seemed to indicate that the tall gentleman was well acquainted with Billy. She had been wondering if he might be a visitor in the neighborhood: somebody's cousin or nephew, perhaps, or a university friend of some local young gentleman attending Oxford or Cambridge. The tall gentleman looked a bit old to still be attending university, however, and it appeared now from his remarks that he must be a local gentleman and not a visitor. Susan cudgeled her brains, trying to think who he might be. But though she scrutinized him closely throughout the dance and even asked one or two leading questions, he parried them so skillfully that by the end of the dance she was no wiser than before. She was meditating what further measures she might take to solve the mystery when Minnie came hurrying up in a state of great excitement.

"Oh, Susan," she cried, grasping Susan's arm eagerly and in the process revealing to all and sundry her friend's identity as well as her own. "Susan, you must come with me right now; *you must*. The squire has arranged the most wonderful surprise for us! He told me just a minute ago, when I was getting a glass of punch with Harry."

"Oh, yes?" said Susan, masking her annoyance as well as she could. "What kind of surprise, Minnie?"

"He has brought in a Gypsy to read our fortunes! Well, not just *our* fortunes, of course, but all the young ladies'. And so we need to hurry, or else we'll end up having to wait forever for our turn. If we go right now, we can probably be first in line. Do hurry, Susan!"

Susan hesitated, looking indecisively at her partner. "I'm sorry, sir, but it seems I must take leave of you now," she told him. "I hope I shall have the pleasure of talking to you again soon."

Unconsciously she gave these last words a faint questioning inflection. The gentleman smiled warmly and moved a step nearer, addressing her in a voice too low for Minnie to hear. "To be sure you shall. Now that I've found you, I have no intention of letting you slip away so easily. Indeed, I shouldn't wonder if you didn't find me as big a nuisance as Billy before the evening's over!"

"I don't fear that," said Susan, smiling at him rather shyly.

Minnie, meanwhile, had been surveying the tall gentleman with a mixture of interest and approbation. Having verified that he was young, male, and presentable, she registered her approval of these qualities by addressing him in a manner markedly flirtatious. "I beg your pardon, sir, but I don't believe I'm acquainted with you," she said, batting her eyes at him. "Susan, won't you introduce us?"

Susan was most unwilling to fulfill this request, the more so as she had no idea how to introduce a gentleman whose name was unknown to her. In any case, she was saved from doing so by the gentleman himself, who spoke up with a smile. "You may not be acquainted with me, but I believe I'm acquainted with you, ma'am," he said. "Though I never would have recognized you if I had not heard you speak. Can it possibly be—Miss Maxwell?"

Minnie giggled and dropped him a curtsy. "La, sir, you have the advantage of me," she told him, making great play with her eyes over her veil. "I wonder who you can be?"

"We'd better be on our way, Minnie, or we'll miss seeing the Gypsy," said Susan shortly. She felt it was bad enough that Minnie should monopolize Harry all evening without trying to captivate every other decent-looking gentleman at the party. But when she stole a look at the tall gentleman to see how he was reacting to Minnie's flirtatious advances, she saw that they appeared to be making little impression on him. He was looking at her rather than Minnie, and when he saw her looking back, he bowed deeply and took her hand in his own.

"I hope the Gypsy gives you a good fortune," he said, raising her hand to his lips. "And I hope, too, that she gives it to you quickly, so that I may again have the pleasure of your company. *Adios, señorita,* and thank you for the dance."

This address quite restored Susan to good humor. "You're very welcome, I'm sure," she said, and threw him a smile over her shoulder as she left the courtyard with Minnie.

Inside the house, they found the Gypsy holding court in the room known as the Oak Parlor. Several costumed young ladies were already lined up outside the door, and the Squire was bustling about, directing operations with his usual air of energetic good humor.

"There you go, girls," he said, pressing a shilling each upon Minnie and Susan as they joined the others waiting in line. "That's to pay the Gypsy with. A shilling a head was the price we fixed on, so mind you don't let her cozen you into giving her any more. And if you're wearing rings or necklaces or other gewgaws, mind you look sharp to 'em when you're sitting with her. She seemed an honest sort as Gypsies go, but that ain't saying much." He turned to look as a pair of young ladies emerged pink and giggling from the parlor. "Ah, here's a couple of customers just out. Everything satisfactory, I hope?"

"Oh, yes," they assured him with one voice, then exchanged glances and burst into giggles once more. The Squire, smiling indulgently, advised them to go on back to the party. He then turned his attention to the next young lady, a shy damsel who required several minutes of teasing and coaxing before she could be brought to enter the parlor. She came stumbling out a few minutes later as pink and giggly as her predecessors. Two more girls were admitted and discharged in quick succession, and then it was Minnie's turn. She clutched Susan's arm nervously.

"Oh, Susan, I'm so scared," she whispered. "I've never been up close to a real live Gypsy before. And I've never had my fortune told, either, except just with nuts and apple peels and silly things like that. Won't you come in with me, Susan? Those other girls went in together, and nobody seemed to mind."

"Very well," said Susan, not averse to getting an early view of the Gypsy and her fortune-telling technique. She smiled at the Squire, who was holding the door open for them, then followed Minnie into the Oak Parlor.

This room fully deserved its name, being furnished with oaken paneling, oaken floorboards, and a quantity of dark oak furniture. A small square table had been placed in the center of the room, and at a chair behind the table sat the Gypsy. She was a stout, dark woman in her middle years, clad in a purple frock nearly concealed beneath half-a-dozen ragged shawls and scarves. Her graying hair straggled loose about her shoulders, and her eyes were like jet beads in her swarthy face.

She spoke no word as the girls came into the room, but merely indicated the chair placed across from her at the table. Minnie, giggling slightly from nervousness, took a seat in the chair, while Susan seated herself a little distance away on an upholstered settee. The Gypsy's eyes studied Minnie keenly, then flickered to Susan. Susan tried to return her look steadily, but found herself disquieted by the Gypsy's inscrutable jet black gaze.

At last the Gypsy withdrew her eyes from Susan and fixed them on Minnie once more. "Let us begin," she said, in a voice that bore a faint, not unpleasing accent. "Please take off your gloves, Miss. It is necessary that I see your hands."

"Why?" asked Minnie, obediently removing her gloves and presenting her hands to the Gypsy. "Why do you need to see my hands?"

"To read your fortune, Miss. Your past, present, and future—all are written here." With a solemn air, the Gypsy touched the palms of Minnie's hands. "I see, for instance, that you are not native to this part of England. Your hands indicate that you have moved to this area in the past—in the near past, I would say, within the last year or two, perhaps."

"That's right," breathed Minnie, regarding the Gypsy with awe. "Oh, but that's wonderful, ma'am. What else do you see?"

Susan, on the settee, smiled skeptically to herself. It

was true that Minnie had moved to Roxbury in the not-too-distant past, but this was a fact that might have been deduced quite easily from her North Country accent without reference to her hands. Any belief that Susan had entertained about the genuineness of the Gypsy's powers vanished. She was quite convinced now that the woman was a charlatan, and she listened with interest to see what threadbare predictions she would produce next.

"I see love here, and much of romance," continued the Gypsy, scrutinizing Minnie's hands. "You have many suitors, no?" Minnie giggled, tacitly admitting the fact. The Gypsy smiled slightly and went on in a dramatic voice. "There will be many gentlemen who will seek your hand, but to one only shall your heart be given."

Susan rolled her eyes at this. Anyone looking at Minnie might know she had plenty of suitors. And the last part of the Gypsy's prediction was patently incorrect, for Minnie was apt to fall in and out of love with the greatest of ease. By her own admission, she had previously given her heart to several gentlemen in the North Riding before moving to Roxbury and bestowing it on Harry.

"One gentleman, and one gentleman alone shall win your heart," repeated the Gypsy solemnly. "I see a gentleman tall, dark, very handsome—"

"Dark?" said Minnie in disappointment. "Are you quite sure he is a *dark* gentleman, ma'am?"

"—I see a gentleman tall and dark who will for a time engage your thoughts, but it is a fair gentleman who will win your heart," said the Gypsy smoothly. "A fair gentleman, gay and laughing and very handsome."

"Yes, that's Harry," said Minnie delightedly. "You are quite right in describing him, ma'am—and right about the dark gentleman, too, now that I think about it. I had almost forgotten, but back when I lived in Yorkshire I used to fancy myself in love with Lord Julian Fontaine, and *he* was a tall, dark gentleman. You remember my telling you about Lord Julian, I'm sure," she said, turning to address Susan. "I used to be quite wild about him, but of course that was a long time ago, when I was only a child. It was not until I met Harry that I was ever really in love."

"Of course," said Susan gravely. Her voice must have betrayed her amusement, however, for the Gypsy gave her a brief, searching look before turning her attention again to Minnie's hands.

The remainder of the Gypsy's predictions were trifling stuff. She foresaw a mild illness to one of Minnie's near relations, which she assured the anxious Minnie would result in no lasting ill effects. She saw also a letter which would shortly arrive from an acquaintance Minnie had not heard from in several months, and a journey which she would be taking in the near future in company with someone close to her. Minnie joyfully confirmed this latter prediction, saying her father meant to take her to London the following week.

"It's wonderful how you can know such things, ma'am," she declared, as she rose from her chair. "I cannot thank you enough for the warning about Grandmama. I'll make sure she wraps up well when we leave here, and that the maids put a warming pan in her bed tonight before she retires. She *is* rather susceptible to colds, no doubt about it."

Having paid the Gypsy her shilling and disobeyed the Squire's injunction by pressing an additional sixpence upon her—the last money she possessed in the world—Minnie turned to Susan.

"Would it be all right if I went back to the party now?" she asked. "I must tell Harry what the Gypsy said about my future husband. Or do you want me to stay with you while your fortune is read?"

"No, you go on, Minnie," said Susan, seating herself

in the chair her friend had just vacated. "I'll be fine by myself."

As soon as Minnie had gone, Susan looked across the table at the Gypsy. The Gypsy looked back at her steadily, her eyes black and unblinking as chips of obsidian. Once again, Susan found herself disquieted by that impassive regard, but she was determined not to show it. "Aren't you going to tell me my fortune?" she asked.

The Gypsy did not answer the question immediately, but contemplated Susan a moment longer. "Certainly I will tell your fortune, Miss," she said at last. "I only ask myself—will you believe it if I do?"

"No," said Susan frankly.

She thought the Gypsy would be offended, but to her surprise the woman laughed, showing teeth startlingly white in her swarthy face. "You are honest, at least," she said. "Not very polite, perhaps, but honest."

"I'm sorry," said Susan, struck by compunction. The Gypsy laughed again, however, and shook her head.

"No, Miss, you need not be sorry. I do not mind your being honest. It is a commendable quality, honesty. We will be honest together, yes?" Leaning forward across the table, she addressed Susan in a confidential voice. "Between you and me, then, I admit that such fortunes as I gave your little friend a minute ago are worth—just so much as that." She snapped her fingers dismissively. "It is nothing to guess that such a young lady has many admirers, or that she will soon receive a letter or go on a journey. A baby could read such a fortune as that. But that is the kind of fortune the young lady wants, so I give it her, and she is happy. And that is not a bad thing, no?"

"I suppose not," said Susan grudgingly.

The Gypsy smiled at her. "But you must not think that because I give your friend such a fortune, that is the only kind of fortune I can give." In a dramatic gesture, she laid a hand on her shawl-covered bosom. "Me, I have the gift of seeing the future—the true gift of second sight, which is given to very few," she told Susan proudly. "Not always can I see the future, nor, alas, it is given me to see it very clearly. But a glimpse, now and then, is vouchsafed to me of events that are and are to come."

"Oh, yes?" said Susan politely. She did not fool the Gypsy, however, who gave her a sharp look and then smiled in resignation.

"Still you do not believe," she observed. "That is not wonderful, that, for you have no way of knowing that I do not make up stories as I did before. But I am speaking the truth now, I promise you—and I mean to prove it to you, if I can."

Reaching across the table, she took Susan's hands in hers. Susan expected she would examine them as she had done with Minnie, but instead she merely held them in her own while gazing into Susan's eyes with an intensity that was disquieting. At last she began to speak, in a low, conversational voice.

"You are looking for something," she said. Susan looked at her quickly but said nothing. "You are looking for something," repeated the Gypsy with conviction. "And you will find it—yes, assuredly, you will find it, Miss. Indeed, the thing you seek is already within your grasp, but you do not see it. You are looking in the wrong place. Attend me well, Miss: it is necessary that you should look a little closer to home."

"Oh," said Susan, taken aback.

The Gypsy smiled at her and went on, in the same conversational tone. "You are very young," she said. "It is natural that the eye of youth should be dazzled by gilt and pinchbeck—"

"I'm almost nineteen," said Susan, a trifle offended.

The Gypsy laughed. "You are young," she repeated

firmly. "It is because you are young that you are experiencing difficulties at present. When you are older, you will come to see what is and is not important, and then—ah, then I have no doubt that happiness shall come to you." Releasing Susan's hands abruptly, she said, "That is all. You may go, and tell the next young lady to come in."

A little startled by this sudden dismissal, Susan got to her feet. "Thank you," she said awkwardly. "Thank you very much, ma'am." Halfway to the door, she remembered the shilling the Squire had given her and returned to lay it on the table in front of the Gypsy. "Thank you," she said again. Moved by an impulse she did not fully understand, she then removed the ring from her left hand and laid that on the table, too.

The Gypsy accepted the ring and shilling without comment but with a vestige of a smile on her swarthy face. Susan dropped her a slight curtsy, then turned and hurried out of the room, certain that her face must be fully as red as that of any of the young ladies' who had preceded her.

Four

Susan was thoughtful as she rejoined the party in the courtyard. She had not much time to indulge in this mood, however, for before she had advanced three steps she was seized on by Minnie, who was eager to discuss with her the Gypsy's amazing prescience.

"Wasn't she wonderful, Susan? I still can't get over how she described Harry, exactly as though she had seen him. And then, the way she knew about my moving down here from Yorkshire, and about Papa taking me to London next week! It was positively uncanny. Did she give you a good fortune, too?"

Susan found herself curiously reluctant to discuss the fortune the Gypsy had given her. "Yes, pretty good," she said evasively. "Not as specific as yours, though, Minnie."

"Yes, mine *was* very good, wasn't it?" said Minnie, pluming herself a little. "That's why I couldn't resist giving the Gypsy an extra sixpence on top of that shilling the Squire gave us. I knew I ought not to, but it was so amazing how she knew all those things about me! And such a relief to hear that Harry really is to be my future husband. I have been so afraid that his papa would make him offer for some rich titled London lady instead. It was worth every penny I had to hear I needn't worry about that any more." Minnie giggled suddenly. "And upon my word, I really did give her every penny I had,

Susan! It's a mercy I spent most of my money this afternoon when we were out shopping, isn't it?"

Susan nodded. "Yes, it is. That Gypsy had quite a way with her. I made up my mind beforehand that she was a fraud, but by the time she was done I was just like you, ready to give her every penny I had. Unfortunately, I hadn't any money with me, so I ended up giving her my ring instead." She looked down at her left hand, now bereft of its ornament. "I can't imagine how I came to do anything so silly."

"What, that pretty little gold ring you bought just this afternoon at Rudges'?" exclaimed Minnie. Grabbing Susan's hand, she verified that there was no ring on the third finger, then looked at Susan with an expression of mingled awe and reproach. "Oh, Susan, how could you? Why, that ring cost you nearly a pound!"

"I know it," said Susan, pulling her hand away. "It was very silly of me, but I can buy another one with my next month's allowance, perhaps. Don't tell anyone about it, will you?"

Minnie promised she would not, and the chances of her keeping this promise were improved a moment later by the arrival of Harry on the scene, which served to give her thoughts quite a different direction.

"Hello, Harry," she said, greeting him with a flirtatious smile. In a loud aside to Susan, she added, "I am extremely vexed with Harry, Susan. I told him what the Gypsy said, but he only laughed and said I mustn't put too much faith in the predictions of an old beggar-woman. Didn't you, you wicked man?" she continued, turning back to Harry.

"Aye, that I did," said Harry, smiling down at her fondly. Susan observed his expression with a faint feeling of envy. Her envious mood was dissipated a moment later, however, by a light touch on her shoulder. Turning, she found herself confronted by the tall gentleman

in the black domino who had been her partner during
the last dance. Rather to Susan's surprise, Harry also
seemed to recognize this gentleman, for he greeted him
as an old acquaintance. The gentleman returned his
greeting, nodded pleasantly to Minnie, and then turned
to Susan.

"You see I have kept my promise, *señorita,*" he said,
taking her hand and bowing over it. "I hope I may have
the pleasure of dancing with you once again?"

Susan assented to this proposition with shy pleasure.
The sight of him had acted as a tonic on her spirits, and
she found she could now view even the sight of Minnie
flirting with Harry with tolerable complacency. Glancing at that couple, she observed that their flirtation was
proceeding along the usual lines. Harry, with obvious
enjoyment, was assuring Minnie that he was not wicked
at all, while Minnie was asserting warmly that he was.

"Indeed, you are quite horrid, Harry," she told him
with a beguiling pout. "If you had been there to hear
the Gypsy yourself, you would not dare to sneer at her
predictions in that odious way. You're a—a—oh, I can't
tell you what you are. You're a wicked, scoffing, unbe-
lieving man, that's what you are."

"A regular Giaour, in fact," suggested the tall gentleman, who had been listening to this exchange with
amusement. Both Minnie and Harry looked at him
blankly. "A Giaour, like in Byron's poem," he explained.
"And very appropriate, now I think of it. You have your
Leila with you, after all."

Both Minnie and Harry continued to look at him
blankly. "I think perhaps you've got the wrong sow by
the ear there, old fellow," said Harry, voicing what was
obviously the opinion of them both. "Mean to say, I'm
a Hussar, not a—whatever it was you called me."

"A Giaour," repeated the tall gentleman, with commendable solemnity. Susan bit her lip, trying not to

smile. "Giaour is another word for an unbeliever, you know," he went on in a kindly voice. "And of course it is also the title of Byron's famous poem about the tragic romance between a Christian gentleman—a giaour, by Eastern standards—and a lady in a Mussulman's harem. And seeing that your lady is in Eastern dress, it all seemed very apposite."

"Oh, aye, just so," said Harry, with the air of one too polite to disagree. Turning to Minnie, he offered her his arm. "Care to dance this next set with me, Minnie?" Or would you rather go outside and take a look at the bonfire? They ought to be burning the Hallow Man pretty soon."

"The Hallow Man?" repeated Minnie with interest. "Whatever in the world is that, Harry? I never heard of such a thing."

"Just an old tradition," said Harry with a shrug. "There's not much in it, really."

Seeing that Minnie was not much enlightened by this speech, the tall gentleman saw fit to intervene once more with a word of explanation. "Every year on All Hallows' Eve, the villagers make up a bundle of straw shaped like a man and burn it in the Squire's bonfire," he told Minnie. "It's a custom that's been practiced in Roxbury as long as anyone can remember."

"Indeed," said Minnie, looking impressed. "It sounds very quaint and picturesque."

"It is," said Susan, smiling at her. "Very quaint and picturesque—and probably very pagan, too. Mr. Nesbit thinks so, at any rate! I suppose the custom of burning the Man probably did have pagan origins, but whatever meaning it had was lost centuries ago. It's just a tradition now, and no one except Mr. Nesbit has ever objected to it."

"Oh, Mr. Nesbit," said Minnie, dismissing the curate with a sniff. "He's horridly strait-laced about nearly everything, isn't he? I think your Hallow Man ceremony sounds delightful, and I should like very much to see it." She looked at Harry appealingly.

"Then you shall," said Harry, with gallant promptitude. "We'll go out and take a look right now."

"Would you like to go out, too?" the tall gentleman asked Susan. "Or would you rather stick to our first arrangement and dance?"

Susan, after a moment's consideration, decided that she would prefer to go out and see the Hallow Man burned. The tall gentleman gave her his arm, and together the four of them left the courtyard and went out onto the terrace, where the villagers were holding their revel around the bonfire.

The party outside was much larger than the one contained within the courtyard, and much less formal in its trappings. A few of the guests were costumed, but most were dressed in their ordinary Sunday clothes. These were colorful enough to suit any but the most critical beholder, however, and it was notable that the male guests were quite as colorful as the female, not being limited to the austere garb obligatory to gentlemen. Farmers in embroidered smocks mingled with girls in ribboned caps and print dresses and made altogether a gay spectacle as they stood in groups about the bonfire or romped their way through an exuberant country dance.

Dancing here was not the orderly pastime that it was in the courtyard. There was a good deal of loud-voiced banter between partners; a good deal of laughter and flirtation, and even a certain amount of kissing. One particularly brash couple stood locked in each other's arms at the edge of the dance floor, oblivious to the jests and catcalls of their companions around them. Susan averted her eyes from this couple in some haste, and in doing so encountered the eye of a stout country swain.

He returned her gaze with interest, then advanced toward her with a wide grin on his round, red face.

"Ah, here's a sweet piece," he said, hailing Susan in a boisterous and slightly drunken voice. "Will ye dance with me, pretty lass?" Not waiting for an answer, he grasped Susan's arm and began to pull her toward the dance floor.

"No, I thank you, sir," said Susan, trying to free her arm from his grasp. "I do not wish to dance just at present."

Both her protests and her attempts to free herself were unavailing, however. She would certainly have been removed to the dance floor by her bucolic admirer had not the tall gentleman reached out and caught him by the wrist.

"I beg your pardon, sir, but the lady does not wish to dance," he said. He spoke quietly, but something in his voice must have carried conviction, or perhaps it was only the grasp of his hand on the man's wrist. In any event, the countryman immediately let go of Susan's arm and took himself off, rubbing his wrist and muttering under his breath.

Having seen him off, the tall gentleman then resumed possession of Susan's arm himself. As they continued on their way along the terrace, Susan gave him a shy smile. "It seems I must thank you for rescuing me once again, sir," she said. "I hope you will not be obliged to do so all evening!"

"Even if I am so obliged, it shall be my pleasure," said the tall gentleman, smiling back at her. "I would rather have the pleasure of your conversation, however. Shall we find some place we can sit and talk, while we wait for the Hallow Man to put in an appearance?"

Susan agreed to this plan, and they seated themselves on the low wall of the terrace, not far from the refreshment table. Minnie and Harry did not follow their example, but instead went over to join the crowd around the bonfire. Susan watched them idly for a few minutes, but soon Harry's tall figure and Minnie's round one were lost from view among the other revelers. Susan turned her attention back to her companion and found he was regarding her with a pensive expression.

"Our friends apparently prefer to do their waiting by the fire," he said. "I hope it doesn't make you uncomfortable to sit out here alone with me?"

"Oh, no," Susan assured him. It was an odd fact, but she found herself not at all intimidated by her present situation. Excited, stimulated, and intrigued, yes—but she had no doubt that she was perfectly safe in the tall gentleman's company. With a smile, she added, "Indeed, I am not sorry that we are alone, for now I can tell you that I, at least, appreciated your joke about Leila and the Giaour. It is a pity that the rest of your audience was so little amused!"

The tall gentleman smiled. "Yes, that joke did fall rather flat, didn't it? I ought to have known better than attempt a joke with a literary reference around Harry. He never opens a book, unless it's the *Turf Register* or *Stud Book*. But that's not to discount him in any way. He's as good a fellow as they come; just not at all bookish, as he himself would say."

Susan made no immediate answer. The tall gentleman had spoken casually, but his words had started the germ of an idea in her mind, an idea that was startling in its implications. It was necessary for her to reflect a minute or two before she could put her thoughts into words.

"Perhaps that is part of the reason Harry and Minnie get on so well," she ventured at last, in a voice of discovery. "Minnie scarcely ever opens a book, either. She never made it past the first chapter of *Evelina*, which I had thought the most entertaining book in the world. The first time *I* read it, I could hardly put it down, but

Minnie said it was too long, and that she didn't like novels that were 'all letters.' I suppose it is all a question of one's tastes," she went on, with a further air of discovery.

"Yes," said the tall gentleman. "Tastes do vary greatly, to be sure." With a warm look, he added, "I assure you, I feel my good fortune in having found a companion who shares my own tastes to some extent. I have greatly enjoyed my time with you this evening. I hope you will not find it necessary to go rushing off as soon as they've burnt the Hallow Man?"

"Not unless I am obliged to," said Susan. She hoped in her heart she would not be obliged to, for she fully reciprocated the gentleman's sentiments. It had been a very enjoyable evening thus far, even in spite of the minor incidents involving Billy Babcock and the stout countryman. That these incidents had not been allowed to spoil her evening, she had her present companion to thank; and Susan had now a strong desire to stay till the unmasking and see exactly who it was that she owed her thanks to.

She had her suspicions, of course. Ever since Harry had hailed the tall gentleman with a clap on the back and a friendly, "How d'ye do, old fellow?" an idea had been growing in her mind. Perhaps it had taken root even earlier, when the tall gentleman had addressed her in fluent Spanish. But she had tried to dismiss her suspicions at first, for it did not seem possible that the gentleman she had in mind could cut such a dashing figure. Without precisely disparaging him, she had always supposed him cut from the same piece of cloth as such local gallants as Billy Babcock.

It was humiliating now to think she had been mistaken. But mistaken she surely must have been, in some wise. Either she had been mistaken in taking him this evening for a charming, intelligent, conversable gentleman, or (what was infinitely worse) she had been mis-judging him from the beginning of their acquaintance and had been undervaluing his good qualities in the most cavalier way.

Susan looked at her companion. He looked back at her steadily. There was a glow in his dark eyes which might have been merely the reflection of the bonfire, but it caused Susan's heart to beat a little faster. She wanted to ask outright, "Who are you?" but the words would not come. He regarded her silently a moment longer; then, without speaking, leaned down and kissed her gently on the lips. Susan shut her eyes. But they flew open again an instant later, as she regarded her companion with startled comprehension.

"It was you who kissed me at the party last year," she whispered. The tall gentleman nodded, his eyes never leaving her face. He seemed to be waiting for her to say something more. When she did not, however, he merely leaned forward and kissed her again. Again Susan shut her eyes. Her mind was awhirl with surprise, speculation, and wonderment.

It had not, after all, been Harry who had kissed her at the party last year. This realization ought to have been a great disappointment to Susan. She told herself that she ought to feel disillusioned at the very least, to find reality so far removed from her imaginings. Yet she found herself accepting the loss of her most cherished illusions with quite a philosophical spirit. As the tall gentleman's lips continued on her own with a touch at once gentle and insinuating, it was beginning to dawn on her that reality might be even better than her imaginings.

Eventually, after what seemed a very long time, the tall gentleman released Susan from his embrace. She opened her eyes. He was looking down at her, and when he saw her looking back he seemed about to speak. At that moment, however, a shout rose from the direction of the bonfire. Susan looked across the terrace and saw a party of countrymen ceremoniously making their way toward the fire with a life-size straw figure borne high on their shoulders. The tall gentleman saw it, too.

"Ah, they're getting ready to burn the Man," he said. "Shall we go and watch?"

"All right," said Susan. The tall gentleman rose to his feet, then assisted her to hers in a courteous manner. Once she was standing, however, he let go of her arm and took her by the hand instead. Susan made no objection. Hand in hand they crossed the terrace and joined the rapidly swelling crowd around the bonfire.

The countrymen bearing the straw figure were approaching the fire now. The crowd parted silently, making a path to let them through. The mood of the gathering had grown hushed and solemn now, and the fiddlers augmented this mood by leaving off the country dance they were playing and striking up a dirge instead. Susan gripped the tall gentleman's hand tightly in her own. He glanced down at her, then moved a step closer, so that they stood shoulder to shoulder as they watched the spectacle unfold.

Upon reaching the fire, the countrymen lifted their straw burden high in the air and held it there a moment, dramatically. A murmur ran through the crowd. Susan, craning her neck, could just see the figure, a life-size effigy with trunk and limbs of twisted straw and a head made out of a stuffed sack. The sack had been crudely painted in the form of a face, and it seemed to Susan that its features bore a suspicious resemblance to the curate Mr. Nesbit's prim, bespectacled countenance, but about this she might have been mistaken. There was no time for more than a fleeting glimpse, for with a concerted effort the men raised the straw figure high in the air once more, then flung it into the heart of the fire. It instantly burst into flames.

The crowd around the bonfire greeted this spectacle with cheers and applause. Once the straw figure had been reduced to ashes, there was a good deal of back-slapping and hand-shaking among the spectators, as well as a good deal of promiscuous kissing. Susan found herself kissed once more by the tall gentleman, whose kiss she returned enthusiastically. She was also kissed by the Squire, who was bustling through the crowd bestowing smiles, greetings, and handshakes on his humbler-born guests and who insisted on following the tall gentleman's example. Susan had barely subsided blushing from the Squire's embrace when Minnie came flying up with Harry in tow. Minnie's wig and turban were all askew and her veil hung precariously from one ear, but her face was radiant with smiles.

"Susan," she cried, embracing her friend with impetuous fervor. "Susan, you must wish me happy. Harry has asked me to marry him!"

"And did you consent?" inquired the tall gentleman in a voice of anxiety. Minnie threw him a tolerant smile, then turned again to Susan, addressing her in a voice lower but no less euphoric than the one with which she had made her first announcement.

"He has given me his family betrothal ring, see, Susan?" she said, waving a hand ornamented with a handsome diamond in front of Susan's face. "Isn't it magnificent? It makes my poor little pearl ring look positively no-how. And so I was thinking Susan—if you wanted my pearl ring, I thought I would give it to you. You've been such a good friend to me, there's no one I would rather see wear it, and perhaps it would make up a little for your other ring. The ring you lost this evening, you know," she explained, with a conspiratorial smile. "You will take it, won't you, Susan?"

Susan looked down at the ring which Minnie was pressing into her hand. "To be sure I will take it," she said warmly. "It's a hundred times prettier than the ring I lost, Minnie. I will take it and wear it with great pleasure, if you're sure you don't want it anymore."

Minnie assured her she did not, then turned to Harry. "We must go find Grandmama now and tell her the good news, Harry," she told him. "She will be in transports when she hears. I wonder if we could be married as early as Christmastime?"

"I don't see what's to stop us," said Harry, regarding her with indulgent affection. "As far as I'm concerned, the sooner we're buckled, the better."

"Congratulations, Harry," said the tall gentleman, smiling. "I wish you and your bride-to-be very happy."

"And I, too," said Susan. Harry received these congratulations with a bow, looking both pleased and embarrassed.

"Very much obliged to you both, I'm sure. Your servant, Miss Curtis. And yours, too, Richard, old man. Don't forget, we're to meet at my place at ten tomorrow. I'm looking forward to having a try at those coverts out by Miller's farm."

When they had gone, Susan looked at her companion. He sighed, shook his head, and gave her a wry smile. "So much for the concept of masquerade," he said. "Leave it to Harry to let the cat out of the bag. Though I suppose you already had a pretty good idea who I was."

"A pretty good idea," agreed Susan. Despite her suspicions, it was still a shock to hear him speak in the familiar accents of her long-time neighbor and acquaintance, Richard Sheffield. And yet the shock was not at all unpleasant. It was more as if she had discovered that something she had known and taken for granted all her life had proven to be an unexpected treasure.

Richard was looking down at her searchingly. "I thought you had probably guessed who I was, but I wasn't sure," he said. "You mustn't think it was my intention to deceive you, Susan. It was only that—well, somehow I found it easier to express the way I felt about you when I could do it as someone other than myself. The truth is that I have admired you for years, only I've been too shy to say anything about it."

"Have you?" said Susan, gazing at him in wonder. "For years, Richard?"

He nodded. "I don't wonder you're surprised. I hope, however, that you are not displeased. Are you?" He looked down at her searchingly once more. "When you let me kiss you back there, I did hope—but perhaps I'm being presumptuous."

Susan shook her head. "No, you're not being presumptuous, Richard. I won't deny that what you've told me has come as a surprise to me, and perhaps it would be better if I didn't say too much just now, but I *can* say that I have had a wonderful time this evening. And if you should feel like calling on me later this week so we can discuss the situation further . . . well, I shall certainly not discourage you."

A warm smile spread across Richard's face. Catching Susan's hand in his, he carried it to his lips. "I shall call on you tomorrow," he said. Then a thought seemed to occur to him. "Or would it be better to wait a few days? You must know I don't mean to rush you into anything, Susan. Nothing would make me happier than to know you returned my feelings, but I quite understand that you need time to consider your own heart." In a more diffident voice, he added, "I am afraid the news of your friend's engagement must have come as a shock to you. Perhaps I am mistaken, but I have fancied once or twice that you had a—well, rather a partiality for Harry's company, don't you know."

Susan blushed, but her eyes were bright with laughter as she looked up at Richard. "You refine too much upon it, Richard," she said. "It's quite true that I used to admire Harry when I was younger, but now I am older I find my taste is for a different sort of man. And I should be very happy if you would call on me tomorrow."

"Wild horses couldn't keep me away," vowed Richard, and sealed his vow by kissing her once more, to the general approbation of those around them.